True
Confessions
of a
God Killer

THE DREAMSEEKER
FICTION SERIES

On an occasional and highly selective basis, books in the Dream-Seeker Fiction Series, intended to make available fine fiction by writers whose works at least implicitly arise from or engage Anabaptist-related contexts, themes, or interests, are published by Cascadia Publishing House under the DreamSeeker Books imprint. Cascadia oversees content of these novels or story collections in collaboration with DreamSeeker Fiction Series Editor Jeff Gundy as well as at times in consultation with its Editorial Council.

1. Sticking Points
   By Shirley Kurtz, 2011
2. True Confessions of a God Killer:
   A Postmodern Pilgrim's Progress
   By Emily Hedrick 2014

True Confessions of a God Killer

A Postmodern Pilgrim's Progress

EMILY HEDRICK

DreamSeeker Fiction Series, Volume 2

DreamSeeker Books
TELFORD, PENNSYLVANIA

an imprint of
Cascadia Publishing House

Cascadia Publishing House orders, information, reprint permissions:
contact@CascadiaPublishingHouse.com
1-215-723-9125
126 Klingerman Road, Telford PA 18969
www.CascadiaPublishingHouse.com

True Confessions of a God Killer
DreamSeeker Books is an imprint of Cascadia Publishing House LLC
Library of Congress Catalog Number: 2014022141
ISBN 13: 978-1-931038-98-0; **ISBN 10:** 1-931038-98-8
Book design by Cascadia Publishing House
Cover design by Gwen M. Stamm

The paper used in this publication is recycled and meets the
minimum requirements of American National Standard for Information Sciences—
Permanence of Paper for Printed Library Materials, ANSI Z39.48-1984.1984

Library of Congress Cataloguing-in-Publication Data
Hedrick, Emily, author.
True Confessions of a God Killer : a Postmodern Pilgrim's Progress / Emily
Hedrick.
    pages cm. -- (DreamSeeker Fiction Series ; Volume 2)
    Summary: "This allegorical novel tells of a young woman's journey through the
need, after God became sick, to kill the God she knew to make space for a God
beyond the cherished notions through which she had imprisoned God." "[sum-
mary]"-- Provided by publisher.
    ISBN 978-1-931038-98-0 (5.5 x 8.5 trade pbk. : alk. paper) -- ISBN 1-
931038-98-8 (5.5 x 8.5 trade pbk. : alk. paper)
    1. Christian fiction. I. Title.

PS3608.E334T78 2014
813'.6--dc23

2014022141

20 19 18 17 16 15 14   10 9 8 7 6 5 4 3 2

For Michelle

Contents

True Confessions of a God Killer

Prologue

For as long as I could remember I had lived in a dream that was not my own. It was an inherited dream, unknowingly passed on by those before me and those before them, creating a world that seemed as real to me as any other simply because it was the only world I had known.

Perhaps I had once known what it meant to be awake, but the pleasantness of the dream kept me sleeping in comfort. The dream was secure. I lived in a safe town with definitive walls to protect me, narrow streets that guided me where I was told I was supposed to go, and the ongoing approval of those around me. But the dream came with a cost. To continue living in safety, I had to accept the dream and carry it forward as my own.

The dream was *not* mine nor was I able to accept it. The longer I slept, the more sinister it became until I found myself living in a nightmare. This is the story of how I began to wake up.

The Murder

Chapter 1

I spent my childhood happily enclosed within the thick, forbidding walls that surrounded our town. The dream I lived in was built for security. Not only did the massive town walls speak to our desire for safety, but the very nature of the town's systems spoke to it as well. There was a simple reason for this: the outside world was dangerous. I was constantly being told stories of how our ancestors had once lived there in anguish.

"We were a lost group of wanderers, tormented, alone. We didn't know how to live. It was a dark world," some of the older members of our town would say. "But God found us. He saved us. He gave us this town. As long as we stay here and listen to what God says, we'll be safe." And that was our life's calling: to stay safely within the town, unperturbed by what lay beyond it.

Sometimes people would leave the town in search of something more. One of two things would happen to them: They'd either return with stories of the dangerous outside, thanking God for his forgiveness because he was willing to take them back, or we'd forget about them because they'd never return.

The people of our town understood that the walls we had built could not keep us safe from everything. There was a danger lurking within our very town that threatened us daily: ourselves.

After all, we came from that dangerous outside world. We possessed the very evil from which our walls attempted to protect us. Therefore it was not our walls that were the ultimate safety. Rather, God was the most essential part of our protection. God was the one who saved us from the outside world in the first place. He brought us to the town, helped us build the wall, and was saving us from ourselves ever since. From birth we were taught that as long as we continued to obey him and develop personal relationships with him, we would be protected not only from the outside world but from ourselves as well.

For the most part I accepted these stories. I decided at a young age that I would be faithful to our town and to God. Nothing would be able to entice me to leave the secure walls that kept me safe. But even as I made these promises to myself, I caught glimpses of the suffocating dream that was dictating my existence.

I struggled to find God for a large part of my childhood. It was disturbing to me that I was supposed to be in a personal relationship with God, yet he was nowhere to be found. I was told that God was in charge of the town, but every time I poked my head into the offices of the town hall, all I saw was the Man of God and his council discussing what God wanted for our town, with God nowhere to be seen. Every week when the town gathered for our special meeting time when we thanked God for all he had done for us and listened to what the Man of God had to convey to us from God himself, I looked throughout the group of people, trying to see if God was hiding somewhere, but still he was nowhere to be seen.

"Why do we sing and talk to God if he's not here?" I would sometimes ask out of genuine confusion. After the looks I received from the people around me, I learned not to ask that question anymore. It seemed as if everyone knew where God was except for me, and the more questions I asked, the less I belonged.

Despite my efforts at self-containment, my questions got worse. By the time I was twelve I still hadn't managed to keep myself from asking too many questions during our citizenship education classes. One day our teacher came in with a copy of our town's Code of Conduct, a list of rules derived from the larger book, "the Story," given to us by God, which our town depended on for instruction. It seemed as if she was holding an unending roll of paper. I can still feel the way my stomach dropped in devastation along with the bottom of the roll as it dropped to the floor.

"Does God really get angry so easily?" I ventured timidly, staring in awe at the fat roll of paper yet to be unraveled at our teacher's feet. I had recently decided that maybe I couldn't find God because I was doing something wrong, and if I tried harder to have a good relationship with him, he'd actually show up. By the looks of the daunting list, my hypothesis was probably correct. However, fixing my problem would be impossible.

She gave me a little, knowing smile. "I wouldn't say he gets angry as much as he gets concerned for us. This," she said, shaking the list at me and causing the unrolled part on the floor to make a path of legalism to my chair, "is about sin. Sin gets in the way of our relationship with God. When we sin, sometimes it keeps us from seeing the Truth."

I wrinkled my brow. "The Truth?" I asked. I could sense the stares of other students around me. Perhaps I was going too far. I just wanted to understand so that I could please God.

"Yes, we know the Truth. That's why we're here. We're committed to the Story, and we will tell others about it so they can see the Truth and be saved. Then they will be able to have a good relationship with God and we can continue living safely in our town."

My head was beginning to hurt, but that didn't stop me from asking one last question, "What *is* the Truth? I know that God saved us, but. . . . "

Our teacher, who seemed so kind a moment before, gave me a stern look. Clearly no more questions would be tolerated. The chastisement stung a little, and I made certain to look exceptionally interested in what she continued to say as I pondered what had just occurred. To have a good relationship with God, I was supposed to know what the Truth was and be completely sure of it.

After a time, I realized that nobody actually knew what the Truth was, but they all seemed to believe in it wholeheartedly. When I attempted to ask about it, I was told that this unquestioning belief was a sign of maturity called "faith."

The longer a person lived in the town, the more terms they came up with to describe the Truth. People had different ways of talking about it. Some people would focus very intently on the Story, saying that it was our link to God's will and we had to follow everything it said. Others would talk about how God saved us out of his abundant love and they had no other option but to return his love. It was a language that took awhile for me to learn, but as I continued to grow up, I found my own way of speaking it, and it wasn't long before I discovered the profound Truth they spoke of and found a way to believe in it as well.

Although I still hadn't found God the way I wanted to, I grew to love him through the way people talked about him. I often imagined the way his eyes sparkled as he looked upon the people he loved. Sometimes I would even talk to him, hoping he could hear me. I was taught to thank him for all the good things in my life and ask him for help when things were going badly. Overall it was a satisfactory relationship minus the fact that God was my imaginary friend more than a real being. Over time I learned to accept my own hope that I might be interacting with God rather than searching for him, and for several years this approach satisfied me.

The condition - Jerusalem
How to cope
    Violence   Sacarii Sophorii
    withdrawal   Essenes
    Non-violent - confront

Chapter 2

All of this changed, however, the day I heard God's cough.

At first I thought I had imagined it. We were in one of our weekly town gatherings, and the Man of God was speaking about God's newest plans for our town. The group assembled was large enough that anyone could have been feeling slightly under the weather, but something inside me assured me that this was no regular cough. It was God's cough.

"Did you hear that?" I asked someone next to me.

"Hear what?"

"God. I think he's sick or something. I thought I heard him coughing."

"That makes no sense. God can't get sick. He's God. It's probably just someone nearby."

It occurred to me in that moment that I had never officially heard God before this instance let alone seen him so I had no real authority to say that God was coughing—especially amid all the more mature townspeople at the gathering. I was only eighteen. I still had so much to learn about God in comparison to the majority of the town. Perhaps I just needed to ignore what I heard. I sat through the rest of our time together turning a deaf ear to the cough, and when it was finished, I tried to forget my confusion.

Within a few days I had almost succeeded, but suddenly I heard God coughing again! This time it was at a weekly Story study group I had been attending. One of the members of the group had been talking about the different things God had been revealing to her that week when I heard God sputter a bit and attempt to clear his throat. For a second, I thought he was about to say something, but then I realized it was just his cough.

Throughout the next few weeks, God began coughing more and more frequently, and I started to become genuinely worried. I had never heard God before I heard his cough, and I had no indication that my senses were speaking truth other than that gut feeling in my stomach that wouldn't go away. If only I could see God coughing! If only some other person could assure me that I wasn't crazy. And what if I was? God couldn't possibly be getting sick. This was unacceptable! I had only one place to go: my mother.

My mother and I had a strange relationship when it came to things related to God and the Story. Most of the time, we didn't discuss it. I know I embarrassed my father, an upstanding citizen of the town, when I asked too many questions. He preferred to pretend that my questions were non-existent, and I learned at an early age to support that illusion. This meant that any time I did talk to my mother about it, it was in secret, and while she was compassionate in listening to my questions, she always tried to steer me back to the narrow paths the town had provided me with my entire life.

I approached her when I knew my father wasn't at home. She was cooking dinner.

"Mom," I began as she put a pot of water on to boil. "I'm concerned about something."

She turned to face me with a small smile, unaware of the strangeness of what I was about to tell her.

"I've been hearing God a lot recently."

Her face brightened. "Well, that's wonderful!"

I shook my head. "No. Well, you see, I don't think I'm hearing what I'm supposed to be hearing."

An intake of breath. My mother never enjoyed these conversations, and they had been getting more frequent lately. "What do you mean?" She said it quietly, carefully, as if she was afraid she'd make the situation worse if she said it too loudly or with too much emotion.

"He's sick, mom. God's sick. I've been hearing him cough."

She closed her eyes for a moment and her small smile returned. "That's silly, dear. God doesn't cough, and besides, I think there might be something going around. Be sure to wash your hands often and you'll be fine."

"Mom, no. I'm serious. I *know* it's God's cough. I can't tell you why. I just know."

She looked at me differently this time, straight into my eyes as if seeing something there that she had forgotten within herself, but she dismissed it with a quick shake of her head.

"I don't want to hear about it again," she said. "It's just a phase. Ignore it and it'll go away." She paused, and then she added, "And keep reading the Story every day like you're supposed to."

I tried to listen to my mother's advice, but the cough continued. Knowing that I couldn't discuss the matter with my parents, I started to ask around to see if other people had noticed. The responses I received were less than encouraging.

"I'm sorry? You think God's getting sick? How is that even possible? Don't talk crazy. This makes no sense."

"You're wrong. God doesn't get sick. God is all-powerful. Suggesting otherwise is going to make your relationship unhealthy. Forget about it."

I was confused. I *knew* that God was developing a nasty cough. I heard it myself. Each day I listened to the advice of my fellow townspeople and ignored what was happening, the cough got worse and louder. While I had started by asking just a few close friends, I was becoming desperate. Soon I was discussing God's developing cough with anyone who would listen.

The answers were still just as disconcerting and vague until one day, a woman came up to me unprovoked and whispered into my ear, "I hear God's getting sick."

I nodded, hoping that maybe she might understand.

She continued, "You may have noticed people don't like to talk about it, but it's not unheard of."

I felt a glimmer of hope rise within me, "Really?"

She bent in even closer to me so as not to be heard, "It's the work of the Evil One."

A shiver of fear ran down my spine. "The Evil One? I thought he was the one that lived outside our town walls."

"Oh, he's sneakier than that. He's constantly looking for people to attack, especially within a town as successful as ours."

I hadn't realized before that moment that a town could be "successful" let alone the fact that ours fit the description.

The woman continued, "Making God seem sick is one of the ways he's trying to attack you. He sees all the potential within you to do good and because you're going on the right path and following God's will, he's trying to make your life miserable."

I was astounded that I was worthy of such personal attention, but people were constantly saying that God had plans for me. If the Evil One truly hated God, whom I loved so much, of course he would want to stop me however he could.

The woman continued, "He's gotten into your mind. He's making you think that God is sick. Hold onto the Truth! You're being lied to. Don't let him play with your mind."

My eyes widened with understanding. Terrified, I asked the woman what to do to make it stop.

"You need to tell him he has no power over you. You know that God is stronger than he is and that God's on your side. Scare him off." With that word of encouragement, she walked away.

For a while, I tried to make the Evil One go away by shouting all manner of things at him. I told him that God was going to show him who was boss because God was stronger. I informed him that I knew about his tricks and that I wasn't going to fall for it. It actually worked for a while. God's coughing stopped, but then I realized I had been yelling so loudly at the Evil One that I couldn't hear God at all. It was almost as if I had been so busy trying to deal with the Evil One that I had forgotten my relationship was with God and not this sneaky trickster.

And who was to say that there really was this evil character? I hadn't seen him. That being said, I had yet to encounter God except in the increasingly frequent coughing fits that only I could hear. My desperation was beginning to overwhelm me. Something needed to change.

Chapter 3

It was time I started looking for God again. Maybe if I actually found him, people would believe me. Even better, maybe if I found him we could find a way to get him to stop coughing. I decided to make some sacrifices in an effort to give myself more time to look for God. Instead of going to one of my weekly group gatherings to discuss the Story, I took the time to scour the streets in search of him by myself. These seemed to be the only times when I didn't hear God coughing. Confused, I tried to discuss it with one of my friend. But she seemed to be more concerned with my behavior than God's health.

"Truly, I don't understand why you're not coming to our group gathering. If you want to get better in touch with God, you need to be spending more time reading and discussing the Story with other townspeople."

I wanted to cry. I didn't know who to believe. God wasn't at the Story study! At least I didn't see him there. And if he was truly sick, then it seemed that I was doing the right thing by not participating in as many activities so I could spend more time looking for him. But everyone seemed to think not only that I was wrong but also that I was damaging my relationship with God. All I wanted to do was to find God and help him get better!

Dejected, I left my friend and found my copy of the Story. Flipping through it, my frustration increased. I could make no sense of the words. I had grown up with them, yet they were foreign to me and of no help in my quest to find God.

Guilt consumed me as I tried to figure out whether or not I should trust myself. Was God truly sick, or was it my fault? Maybe my friends were right. I should be more involved. Maybe more involvement would end up helping God in the end. I decided I would compromise. I would commit myself to all activities in our town, but I would not lie about God's cough.

As time went on, I discovered that I really enjoyed helping out with activities, even if God was getting sick. I was soon leading discussions about the Story and helping the town find new ways to thank God for all that he'd done for us. This put me in an increasingly better mood and gave me hope that one day God would get better. This coughing business was probably just a phase.

One day, a younger girl from the town came up to me and whispered in my ear, "You're the one who says God is sick, right?"

I looked at her, concerned. I knew that people were starting to pay attention to my talk about God, and I didn't want to cause her any unnecessary problems, especially since I was the only one who thought God was sick, and people didn't like it when I brought it up. Yet something inside of me gave me the go-ahead, so I said, "Yes. He has a terrible cough. I don't understand it." Feeling as if I might have been a bit too blunt, I added, "but it's not stopping me from doing all of these wonderful things with the rest of the town. Why do you ask?"

She couldn't meet my gaze. It seemed as if she was ashamed, yet relieved at the same time, "I just wanted to make sure I wasn't alone. That's all." She kicked at the ground a little bit.

"Wait," I said, surprised, "what do you mean? Have you heard God coughing too?" I didn't know how to feel. It was like I was given a ray of hope: Maybe I wasn't crazy. Yet this girl could just be going through a phase like I was, and I needed to encourage her not to think about it so that it would go away.

She still wouldn't look at me. "Well, I haven't heard any coughing, but sometimes I feel a weight in my stomach, like something's not right. And I don't know why." She paused for a moment, then looked up at me, "But we know the Truth, right? Everything really is okay, right?"

I stared at her, conflicted, not knowing what to say, thousands of questions surfacing in my mind. "Have you told anyone else?"

She looked at me with fear in her eyes. "I don't think I'm supposed to," she whispered.

I nodded in understanding. Before I had a chance to say anything further, someone approached me to talk about the next town gathering. As soon as I turned away, she was gone.

Days went by, and I couldn't stop thinking about my conversation with the younger girl. Apparently, I wasn't alone. As I continued contributing to town gatherings and leading Story studies, I started to pay attention to each individual, searching for others like the younger girl, and I began to notice things. There was one man who was always smiling, but when I took the time to actually look into his eyes, I could see a sadness living inside of him like he had a dark secret he kept only to himself.

Some of my women friends from our weekly gathering seemed too easily scared when I brought up certain topics. I wondered if they were secretly eager to address some issues but not sure if they were allowed, so they would automatically start talking about the Story or God's love instead.

I often saw the younger girl with the weight in her stomach sitting quietly next to a group of sullen boys during our town gatherings. They just sat there with eyes glazed over, waiting for us to finish. No, I was certainly not alone.

I felt like I needed to do something. I needed to send out the message to these individuals that they weren't the only ones who noticed something was wrong. I needed to let the leaders in the town know that something was going on that was hurting people's relationships with God. I knew that most of the townspeople were unhappy when I brought up certain topics, so I spent a lot of time thinking through how to address these issues without offending the general populace, my thoughts frequently interrupted by the shallow coughing of a God who couldn't breathe.

Soon, my discussion groups and town gatherings subtly mentioned some of the unmentionable things that were going on in people's lives within our town. I got so much positive feedback that I continued slipping in more and more mention of things that were troubling people. I felt good, and I was sure that God was pleased with what I was doing, that perhaps it was helping his cough get better.

Even so, God still *had* a cough. Whenever I wasn't subtly addressing it in my various activities, I tried to forget about it.

Chapter 4

And then it happened. One day, the Man of God was giving us another one of his messages from God when I was finally rewarded for all my searching. I heard the familiar, shallow cough that had become an expected part of town gatherings for me, but this time I focused on where it was coming from, and I found its source.

Surprisingly, I found myself looking toward the Man of God, not directly at him, but ever so slightly behind him. In that moment, my world changed: Standing next to the Man of God was a slight being of white, hands chained together. He looked like an old man, bearded, with eyes that sparkled just as I had imagined. I knew that this was the God I had been searching for the same way I had known that it was God who was coughing.

But to my utter horror, I discovered that the coughing had nothing to do with God being sick and everything to do with God being strangled! Every time the Man of God paused in his speaking, I watched God try to address the group, but the Man of God grabbed him at the throat, suffocating him in an effort to keep him silent while the chains around God's hands kept him from being able to fight back.

I stared, shocked as I realized that for all we knew God may have been trying to speak to us, but we never could have heard him because the Man of God was strangling him.

"STOP!" I screamed. "What are you doing? You're going to choke him to death!"

The Man of God became still and looked at me with utmost concern. Before I was able to fully process what I had just done, he had abruptly ended his talk and discreetly motioned to another man to lead the group in a song of thanks. Then, releasing God from the grip at his throat, the Man of God took the chain attached to God's hands and dragged him toward me.

In truth, I had been avoiding the Man of God because I was still scared that something might be wrong with me, and I was afraid he might notice that I was subtly mentioning things that we weren't supposed to talk about as I led different activities. But as he approached, there was a look of great care and concern in his eyes, and I forgot that he was dragging God, chained, behind him. I reminded myself that this was home. This was the man who could hear God the best out of all of us. He had led me and the people of our small town into better relationships with God for as long as I could remember. He made this place safe. Of course I could trust this man. Of all people, he would be able to help me with my problem.

We walked out of hearing distance from the group, and he motioned for me to sit down on a nearby bench. "You've seemed a little upset lately. Is there something you need to talk about?"

I hesitated, my eyes flickering between the Man of God and the chain he was holding that kept God in bondage. I returned my gaze to the Man of God's face. "Yes. Yes, there is something I need to talk to you about. I'm worried about God."

He seemed genuinely bewildered. "Worried about God? Why are you worried about God?"

I explained everything to him. I told him about the cough. I told him about other people's responses. I even told him about the Evil One and how I couldn't figure out if he was real or not.

"And then you were speaking up there and I realized that God wasn't sick . . . " I paused, perplexed that I trusted the man I had just seen strangling God, "he was being strangled." I furrowed my brow, trying to connect all of the different pieces. They just didn't go together. Something wasn't right.

"And you thought you saw me strangling him? Is that what just happened?" he asked.

"Well . . . yeah," I said, beginning to feel extremely stupid.

"Did anyone else notice me strangling God?"

"Um, well, I didn't . . . I just reacted! Wouldn't you? If you saw someone practically murdering the person you loved most in the world, wouldn't you react immediately?"

"I don't understand."

"How can you not understand?"

"God is all-powerful. I couldn't strangle him."

I thought for a moment, "Yeah. I guess you're right."

"It sounds to me like you have sin in your life."

I stiffened. Sin? But I had been trying so hard to stay away from sin.

He continued, "I've been hearing people in the town say that you've been confusing others and leading them astray. Some have said that you don't respect the older, wiser townspeople and that you've been rebellious and destructive." He looked at me gravely. "Is this true?"

I stared at him, thinking through my interactions with people in the town recently. I had been talking a fair amount about God's cough. But how could I not? I was worried! And others were having problems too. I could see it! What about the young girl with the weight in her stomach? What about the smiling man with the sad eyes?

But maybe it really was the Evil One and I just needed to fight it. If the Man of God was right and he wasn't strangling God, how could I know that anything I saw was real? Maybe I shouldn't have said anything at all. Perhaps I should have just believed people when they told me God was fine, and I was the one having the problems. I was too prideful to listen to the

Truth. And now the people who were closest to me were suffering because of it. What had I done? I really was rebellious. I really was destructive. I really was confusing people and leading them astray.

A tear slipped down my cheek, "Yes," I sniffed, "it's true."

Before I knew what was happening, I had started sobbing uncontrollably. The man of God reached out to comfort me, "I want you know that I love you very much, and I believe that God has great plans for you."

I didn't understand why I was crying so much. This man was here to help me. I was on the right track. We could work together to turn my life around. But right as these thoughts entered my mind, I saw God. With one arm, the man of God was comforting me. With the other, he was holding God in a locked grip. I gasped in horror.

"I was right! You're strangling him! You're strangling God!"

"No. I'm not. That's just what you feel. It's not true. Listen to me." He turned my tear-stained face toward him with his free hand and locked my gaze with his, "I am not strangling God. If you listen to me, we can help you see the Truth."

I couldn't breathe. Something had wrapped around my throat and was preventing the air from passing through. I struggled vigorously to pry it from my neck, but stopped short when I realized I was touching flesh. I hadn't noticed the Man of God's hand slip further down my neck as he turned my face toward his. I was too busy crying to be aware of how vulnerable I was, and now he had swiftly moved from strangling God to strangling me.

Within a moment, I was released and I gasped for air. The Man of God was looking at me again with concern.

"What's wrong with you?" he asked.

My head was swimming. Was it real? Was this man truly just strangling me or had I only imagined it? What *was* wrong with me?

I looked at him, searching his eyes for a trace of rage or guilt, but all I could see was confusion. Neither of us knew what had just happened. There were no answers.

"I'm sorry," I said, "I can't listen to you. I'm too weak. This is what I see. I don't know if you or any of the townspeople would be able to help me change that. I need. . . . " I hesitated, finally letting the reality hit me, "I need to leave." Startled at my own words, I looked at him again and saw my pain and confusion mirrored in his eyes. But in a moment it was gone, replaced with a look meant to keep me and my confusion at a distance. He was about to wash his hands of me.

He stood up. "I don't understand. Nor can I agree with you."

For a moment, a flash of fear surfaced in me, fear that he might try to hurt me again. But the Man of God was done with me. He turned and walked away, leaving God and his chains behind him, an old slave who was no longer of use.

I was on edge, my heart pounding uncontrollably inside my chest: Home was no longer safe. With just one conversation, I had changed from a citizen of this town to a refugee. Apparently, God was being strangled every time I heard him cough, and now, the Man of God had tried to hurt me too. At least, that's what seemed to be the case. Whether it was true or not was beside the point now. I didn't belong here anymore. Not if this was what I saw.

I sat silently on the bench, letting the gravity of this new awareness settle within me. Then, when I could no longer see the Man of God's shrinking form, I got up, and with urgency approached God. He had slumped to the ground with exhaustion. He was sicker than I had thought. How cruel that after all my searching, I found him like this? How many times had he been hurt while he was chained and used for other people's purposes? I took his hand and gently helped him regain his footing. Together, we slowly started making our way down the street toward the edge of town.

We were only a few steps away from the bench when it occurred to me that there were more people in this town than the Man of God. Would he tell the rest of them that I was crazy? Would my friends and family be told? Maybe they had seen what happened as we sat on the bench. Maybe they could tell me if I was crazy or not.

I could feel eyes watching me as I helped God stumble down the street, but I focused my gaze straight ahead. Now that the possibility presented itself, I realized I didn't want to talk to them. I didn't want to know what they had seen. I was too scared of their answers.

Out of the corner of my eye, I saw a group of people approaching us. I recognized them. They were from the weekly Story study that I had led. I could feel a shift in our roles as they came to me. A new leader emerged from the group.

She looked at me, puzzled. "You seem out of sorts" she said. "Is something wrong?"

Now I was forced to ask the question that scared me the most. I braced myself. I told myself that these people were my friends, that I didn't need to be afraid.

"Were you near that bench a few moments ago?" I asked, pointing behind me. The bench was only a few feet away. "Did you see me sitting there? Did you see me talking to the Man of God just now?" I asked.

They all shook their heads.

I let out a sigh. Whether it was of relief or frustration, I wasn't sure. "I'm confused," I said, then hesitated, trying to figure out the best way to word myself. "Listen, do you remember God's cough?"

They nodded, and I could tell already that I wouldn't get through to them. I tried anyway. "He wasn't sick."

They sighed with relief.

"I'm so glad!" said the new leader of the group. "I knew you'd come through it one day!" she paused. "But why are you confused?"

Again, I hesitated. I couldn't tell them my story. I couldn't say that the Man of God was actually strangling God. I gave a vague description instead. "Someone was hurting him," I said. "Someone was strangling him. God is not safe here."

God is not safe here. God is not safe here. The words echoed in a space within me. It felt menacing, as if I had uttered something forbidden. I tried to hush the sound, but instead it got louder and louder inside of me with each repetition. *God is not safe here. God is not safe here.* I needed to run. I needed to scoop God up and make a break for the outside gate.

But the woman had put her hands on my shoulders and was looking at me as if I needed to be disciplined. "There's something wrong with you," she said sternly. "People don't hurt God here. There is nothing wrong with God."

And without warning, the entire group started attacking God.

"No!" I cried. "Can't you see? You're doing it too!" They didn't see. I tried to break into the mob to rescue God, but it was of no use. I was shoved away every time I drew near.

They finally left when God could no longer stand, let alone get up and walk with me out of the town. Tears streaming down my face, I took God's hand and tried to get him upright. It was a futile effort. I had no choice but to carry him.

I was weak with God in my arms and disoriented by the sudden onslaught of violence, but I didn't have the reserve to be afraid any longer. I made my way through the town, the buildings and the streets blurred together amid my tears. It was a different place now, a place I no longer knew.

By the time I reached the town gate, I was using all my strength to put one foot in front of the other. I noted with confusion that no one was there to guard it. What was the wall for anyway? Perhaps it was just the thought of its existence that gave it power. I pulled open the large door just enough so that God and I could slip ourselves through. Exhausted, we collapsed on the other side.

A fresh set of tears streamed down my face as the memory of being suffocated played itself over in my mind. How could this have happened? I stared at the wall behind me, looking at it from the outside for the first time in my life. It was then that I realized its purpose. It wasn't to keep people out or keep people in, though some might believe that to be the case. It was simply there to distinguish who was who. I didn't make sense to them anymore, so I was indirectly forced through the gate. I was an outsider now.

The tears wouldn't stop. I was confused, disoriented, and empty. I needed someone to be there, someone to hold me and tell me I was loved. But the Man of God and all the people I loved were on the other side of that huge wall, and God himself was lying on the ground, helplessly trying to catch his breath again. Desperately, I crawled over to him and took him in my arms. We lay in the grass, intertwined, our tears mixing, our ragged breathing creating a rhythmic song of pain that kept us company as we waited for rest.

Chapter 5

When I regained enough energy, I began to formulate a plan for what I should do next. The one thing I knew for certain was that I didn't want to be an outsider. I *would* go back home. It *was* still home. *I* was the problem. God was the problem. All I needed to do was get God back to normal health. Then I could reenter the town I knew and loved and we could figure out what we needed to do to help me see the Truth again.

For the moment, I needed to locate a place in which God could rest and I could tend to him. Mustering up the strength I had gained, I scooped God up and took a moment to examine the being I had waited my entire life to encounter. His eyes, the eyes I dreamed about for so long, were losing the sparkle I had first imagined. They were tired and weary. Was this truly the God everyone spoke of? Yet I had finally found him! Once I nursed him back to health, he would be magnificent. I turned back toward the gate. "I'll come back," I whispered. "I promise." And with that, I started walking.

It dawned on me within my first few steps that I was now outside the town walls. All the chaos, the evil, the violence discussed in so many testimonies from my childhood would be coming for me. I felt a familiar fear rising within me.

But then I realized that there was nothing new to be afraid of. I knew what chaos, evil and violence were all about. I had already experienced them inside the town walls. The walls had not kept me safe like I was told they would. Besides, God was with me. As I walked, I asked him to help us not run into anyone. I didn't let myself think about how silly it was to ask a sick person to do something for me. After all, he was God.

In half a day's walk, I saw a small, disheveled structure randomly situated in a clear, grassy area. Cautiously, I approached it, wondering about its purpose. As I got closer, I gathered that it was empty and hadn't been used in awhile, but was a much sturdier structure than it first appeared.

I knocked on the door and listened. Nothing. Slowly, I turned the knob. It was unlocked. I was able to step inside.

There was a small bed, a stove, and a table and chairs. Perfect for what I needed. I was still confused as to why this one-room house existed, but was too tired to care. I set God down on the bed, thoughtlessly thanked him for providing this shelter for us, and collapsed on the floor in exhaustion.

I was awakened by a knock on the door. Startled, I cracked the door, and peered through. My mother had somehow managed to follow me. She was carrying a large bag with her.

"Mom?" I opened the door to allow her entry.

She set the bag on the table and looked at me coldly. "What are you doing here? Why did you leave the town? You're not supposed to be here."

I sighed. "I had to get God out of there. He was being hurt."

"You need to come back."

"I can't. Not right now. Can't you see God's sick?" I motioned to the bed.

She shook her head in disgust. "I don't know what kind of a phase this is, but I expect you to get through it as quickly as possible and return home. Do you understand me?"

I was unused to my mother being this blunt, but her plans were identical to mine so I nodded. "You're not supposed to be outside the town either," I said.

"I explained to them that this was an intervention. It was accepted by the council."

"Oh."

"But you're right. I need to be returning. I expect to see you home soon." And with that, she opened the door and marched out.

I peered in the bag. Food. I thanked God for my mother as I rummaged through it. The food was thoughtfully selected. A loaf of bread was on top along with other baked goods and a large amount of canned items that would last for as long as I needed them. Ravenously, I ate a few slices of the bread she had provided, saving the rest of the bag's contents for future use. With the energy it gave me, I began to settle into the little shelter, not knowing how long it would serve as my home.

Time passed. I discovered that caring for a sick God was not a normal activity. The entirety of my life in the town consisted of celebrating God, trying to do what God said, and learning about God. All of these things required God to be healthy. At the moment, he was sick and my experiences in the town left me with no ideas about how to heal him.

For awhile I thought rest would do the trick, so I sat with God and I waited. God didn't change. When it became obvious that doing nothing wasn't working, I tried to figure out what I *could* do. Eventually, and with much experimentation, I figured out how to make God better. It was a process involving great attention, energy, and resources spent on maintaining his health. The key was to give myself completely to God. I had to surrender everything. If I spent any time trying to take care of myself, God would become sicker.

There were different activities of surrender. One of them was singing the familiar songs of thanks and adoration I had been taught in the town. I had refined the art to picking certain aspects of God like his strength or his faithfulness, to focus on and repeating songs about it over and over again until God started fulfilling my words. Sometimes I would sit by God's side, singing to him, telling him how wonderful he was, and after a period of time, God would be able to get up and walk around. We celebrated his progress toward healing together.

Other times, I would sort through all of the different lies people told me about God that wounded him. I tried to remember the things that the Man of God said as I heard God suffocating. Then I would sit by his bedside saying, "These people say this about you, but I don't believe it. They're wrong. God, listen to me. I'll remind you who you are." With that encouragement, God could get up and walk again.

The process wasn't perfect, however. Every time I turned my attention away from God-healing activities, God would get sick again. God's health depended completely on my God-centered actions. At this rate, the only way to get back home with a healthy God would be to sing or talk the whole way. Some days, I played with the idea. Other days, I knew it was impossible.

And even though I had figured out how to temporarily heal God, I felt deeply troubled. I couldn't help but notice that God was losing something every time he got up from the bed. He had healed, yes. He seemed to be stronger, yes. But it seemed the essence of who he was left him, as if each time God got better, any hope of seeing God's eyes sparkle lessened. In confusion, I wrote it off as part of the sickness and tried to pretend that nothing had changed. Still, it haunted me.

Chapter 6

I found different ways to strengthen my resolve. Some of the things I learned in the town were helpful. I remembered the Story about what God had done for our town, how he saved us and gave us a home. I reminded myself that God loved me so deeply I couldn't even fathom it. How could I not love him back? How could I not give him everything I had? There must be more of me to give. One day, God would stay healthy and the two of us would walk back home hand in hand ready to return to the place and the people I loved. One day, God would protect *me*, and nurse *me* back to health. If I held out just a little bit longer, maybe everything would be okay. Maybe this was the last time I'd have to heal him. Maybe. . . .

Yet there was another voice inside me, a voice I was afraid of. It was the part of me that had all the questions. Ever since I had seen God chained up next to the Man of God, I had been contending with one question in particular: How could this pathetic, shriveled up little being be God? He was too weak. He was too helpless, and in all honesty, I couldn't take care of him for much longer.

Each day, I was getting weaker and more exhausted. I despised the fact that I could become so weary when I was doing something so important. I could not reconcile my exhausted, questioning self with the part of me that had been searching for God for so long and had finally found him. I didn't care if he was sick and dying. At least he existed! I didn't want to let him go. The dissonance within me became so pronounced that I had to rip myself apart. I looked at the weary, tired, exhausted part of myself, begging for a break from constant God-tending and said, "Leave. I don't want you here. I'm stronger than this. You're distracting me from what's important. I love God. I will give him everything I have to give. So you go away and never come back."

I sent that part of me away so that I was free to continue taking care of God. But as time went on, I became sad. I started to question whether this was worth it. My depression threatened to overtake me. Nevertheless, I loved God. I needed to do whatever it took to nurse him back to health. Again, I found myself splitting. I looked at the sad, questioning, depressed me and said, "Leave. I don't want you here. I'm stronger than this. You're distracting me from what's important. I love God. I will give him everything I have to give so you go away and never come back."

That part of me left as well. As the days went by, others followed. I sent them all away. Any parts of me who weren't helping take care of God were banished.

It continued to get harder and harder to take care of God. It was taking more time than before, and I was expecting less. I would work for days, worshiping, changing my theology, doing things for God to make both of us feel better. In return, I would have a few minutes of solace, but God's eyes became duller and duller as time passed. Soon it took weeks at a time to get God back to where he should be, and I had forgotten to even look for a sparkle anymore.

One fateful day, as I was sitting by God's bedside, trying to sing to him about how wonderful he was, I opened my mouth and nothing came out. Confused, I tried again. Still, nothing. Then I realized what was going on. There wasn't enough of me left to care. I couldn't sing anymore. I couldn't think anymore. God didn't matter to me any longer. For a long time, I sat in blank silence.

Then I heard a knock on the door. Hoping that perhaps it was my mother with more food, I got up and answered it. I was shocked to discover *me* standing there. I closed my eyes, pinched myself, and opened them again. I was still there.

I stood and stared, waiting for my presence to register, "You don't remember me, do you?" I asked.

"I don't understand," I replied, "Are you a twin? Have we met before?"

I stood there, looking at myself. I looked weary and worn. My face had the look of a person who was starving and hadn't slept in days. I was young, but haggard. What had happened to me? "You sent me away."

I said it with such sadness and longing, it made me second-guess the decision I had made when I split. Perhaps I should have let myself stay. I tried to justify myself.

"You understand, don't you? I had to take care of God. He was first priority. You were getting in the way."

A tear slipped down my cheek, "I know." I could see the sadness in my eyes, like a dark, gray-blue fog that refused to go away "I know you care about him a lot. That's why I left."

I nodded, appreciating the sacrifice I had made.

I continued, "But I never really left. I've always been with you. Every day I watch you trying to nurse God back to health. I've just been hiding, waiting until maybe you might be able to have me back. And now you don't care. Maybe God's not so important anymore. So I thought I'd come out and ask if you would have me." I stopped holding back the tears. Now I was full out sobbing. "I'm sorry I'm such a problem! I can go again if you need me to. I just wanted to check. I really do like you, and I miss you sometimes, well, all the time." My face became downcast. Then I caught myself. "But really, it's okay. I can handle it. I can leave again if you need me to." I looked down, not wanting to make eye contact, waiting for my response.

I stood there for a moment, on the threshold of the small shelter, but also inside of it; waiting for acceptance, and deciding if I could handle having myself back. After a time, I took my hand, guided me into the house, sat me down, and put on some tea, "I think it's worth a try," I said, handing myself a tissue.

I sat with myself and drank my tea in silence.

Then I turned toward the bed to look at God, "He's not doing well at all."

"Yeah, it's been a real struggle. Feels odd that I'm sitting here talking to you. I haven't stopped really, taking care of God. He was so important," I sighed and looked at the feeble figure curled up in the bed.

All of a sudden, the door burst open and I came rushing through, extremely anxious and concerned, "What are you doing? God's lying there on the bed, sick and feeble and you're sitting here drinking tea!"

I was totally appalled at the scene before me. There I was, sitting across from myself, empty mug in hand, with an obviously sick God in the bed, waiting for me to give him strength. God needed me and I was failing him just so I could sit talking to myself over a cup of tea!

Shocked by the entrance of yet another me, I blurted, "I'm sorry, I just don't care anymore. I tried. But when I sing, no notes come out. When I think, nothing makes sense."

"Well fix it!" I yelled back, "This is important!"

"Excuse me!" Yet another me had entered the room. I was beginning to get used to this occurrence. "I don't know why you have to be so pushy. Can't you see she's trying to figure out what's going on? Give her time. She'll get to God eventually."

I ignored myself, "Time is of the essence! God is sick. He needs to be healed. He is top priority. You need to send these folks away. I don't know why you let them back here in the first place."

"She sent you away too, idiot," the fourth me responded, "Maybe *you're* the problem. Maybe she should leave us alone and kick you out."

By this time, I had fully entered the room and finally shut the door, only for it to be opened again by yet another me.

Calmly, I walked into the midst of me's and looked at everyone questioningly, "I'm sensing some tension here. Is everything all right?"

I looked around. One part of me was crying in the corner. Another was standing, hands on hips, in the center of the room, desperately trying to gain control over another part of me standing right in front of me staring me down, trying to defend the part of me sitting across the table from the crying me. This was an extremely confusing situation. God remained silent, curled up in the bed.

Yet another part of myself strolled through the door.

"In answer to your question," I said to the calm part of myself who had entered previously, "everything is not all right. But it's going to be." I gave a stern eye to the group. "Let's all sit down and discuss this over a cup of tea. I'll put another kettle on."

Begrudgingly, I sat down on the floor, the last remaining chair, and the edge of the bed.

The door remained open, and as I prepared tea for myself, more and more parts of myself came to join me. The room was becoming crowded. I counted to 11, then lost track of how many people were present. I began to wonder if there would be enough room for me. Had I really sent all of these parts of myself away in an effort to take care of God?

After everyone was served their tea, I began, "Now, it seems we've been at odds with one another. Which conflict shall we address first?"

This was not the right question. I was immediately answered by almost everyone in the room —and not always in a civil manner. Before I knew what was happening, I was in a huge argument.

"I've had enough of you just leaving me to rot. Who cares about God? Have you taken a look at yourself in the mirror lately? I don't know about you, but I'm exhausted."

"What do you mean you're exhausted? Who cares about you? There are bigger things at stake!"

"And why should I trust what you have to say? I'm sure you have your own agenda."

"Excuse me! Everyone's talking at once! I don't think this is helpful."

"What's going on here anyway? Why are there so many of us? Does this happen to normal people? I think we all might be insane. We should probably do something about that."

"Now, now everyone, settle down. There's a reasonable explanation."

"Stop crying! You're such an attention whore. Stop being melodramatic just so everyone will listen to you! I'm not falling for that crap."

"SHUT UP! WON'T YOU PEOPLE STOP YELLING?"

And all of a sudden, silence—except for what sounded like the sobs of a child. All of me turned to face the corner with the crying me, sitting there in utter distress.

"Please," I sobbed, "please stop. It hurts."

Immediately, I got up to comfort myself. I had been so busy trying to create order and get to the bottom of the problem, I had forgotten about this crucial, fragile piece of me.

I turned to address the crowd. "Listen, some of you are doing an excellent job at making your voice heard." I gave a meaningful look to the part of me that had picked up a chair and was about to throw it across the room. "But there are others who are crucial, and not strong enough to get their message across. You all know who you are. Can we hear from some of the smaller voices?"

Everyone sat down again. I hadn't realized that the entire room was in an outrage. As I watched myself put the chair down, I heard the crunch of broken mug beneath my foot. Furniture was strewn everywhere, and it looked like one of the parts of myself had acquired a black eye. I was starting to feel quite ashamed at the mess I had made. There was a bit of a shuffle until everyone was settled.

A heavy sigh, and then I spoke from my spot on the floor underneath the window, "I don't think you really need to *hear* anything. Have you truly experienced yourself lately? Have you paid attention? Take a look at yourself. What do you see? Take a moment to just be. How do you feel?"

There was no mirror in the shelter, but I didn't need one. I was sitting right there, taking up the entire room. So I listened to myself, and I looked. I took everything in, not just focusing on one piece of me, but rather the split and scattered whole. What did we all have in common?

I saw exhaustion. It was a dark haze, like a shadow, an unseen but present part of all of me. There were bags under my eyes, eyes that expressed suppressed pain, sadness, loneliness. There was an ache for rest behind them that I had not acknowledged in my frenzy to keep God alive. For the first time, I listened to that ache: slowly, I allowed my eyes to close. It had been so long I had forgotten what it felt like to be swallowed by that comforting dark that promised protection if only for a moment.

I breathed in, taking in the air in the room, the exhausted dark haze, the hopelessness, the sadness and pain of each piece of me sitting there after I had sent myself away so many times. There was frustration, loneliness, fear, doubt, and . . . anger, actually. Anger that I had been pushed aside, abused even, for the purpose of caring for something as pathetic as God.

I waited, allowing all of these things to make their presence known to my body, daring myself to accept them. When I did, I let out a slow exhale, ridding myself of the need to neglect who I was to serve a greater purpose, the need to believe the lie that I wasn't important, the need to pretend. Funny how embracing the dark in me could be so cleansing.

Slowly, I opened my eyes again. The room was darker and the air thicker with hopelessness than before. I had let it become part of me . . . no, it had always been there. I was just admitting it this time. Perhaps the darkness should have scared me, but I was too tired to panic. Instead, I looked up at the rest of me, which had, in that short time, shrunk. The group had downsized by at least half. I knew they hadn't left. Rather, they had merged with each other. Now that I had confronted what I had been trying to hide, I had begun the journey to wholeness.

"I'm dying aren't I?" I asked the room, "I'm working myself to death."

The whole room nodded, all of me in agreement, though some nods were vigorous and others more reluctant.

"What am I to do?"

From the windowsill I caught my gaze, the dark haze swimming freely in my eyes. "You can't go on like this." I looked toward the bed. "You need to leave him. You need to let him die."

A sharp intake of breath and everything I had let go of moments before came rushing back into my body. I felt my defenses return. The thought of leaving God was too much for me to handle, "NO!" I cried in utter horror, "how could you even suggest such a thing? He needs me!"

"He's taking all of your strength. You have nothing left."

"You don't understand. He *is* my strength. Don't you remember?" I sang one of my worship songs to try to remind myself, but didn't get very far. Exasperated, I continued trying to explain, "Without him, I'm nothing!"

"He's dying."

My arguments were growing weaker. "I don't care. I've healed him before. He can get better."

"You'll die of exhaustion first."

I knew I was right. I could sense myself fading away; I had seen it. But I had spent so much time and effort taking care of God, I couldn't give up now. Maybe this was just a test to see how truly devoted I was. Maybe God wasn't actually this sick. And anyways, I'd been told so many times that God would never give me more than I could handle. No, I couldn't abandon him. I turned to myself resolutely. "I will *not* leave him."

A heavy sigh, "Are you going to send us away again, then?"

I thought for a moment. "No. I need you. All of you. We're going to make this work, together."

I nodded solemnly in response. It had been decided.

Chapter 7

Though I decided to stay with God, I was determined to make some positive changes. The first was that I made sure every part of me was allowed to stay. This was hard, because I had been living only with selected, acceptable parts of me for so long. Eventually, I made a compromise. If I felt part of me was getting in the way and I was unable to handle it, I'd ask myself to leave for a period of time and come back as soon as I thought I could manage it. This worked fairly well.

Most of the time, I was "by myself" so to speak. I could merge most parts of me into one. It would only seem as if there was one me in the room, taking care of God. However, when it was necessary, I would allow other pieces of myself to split off. Sometimes when I was feeling overwhelmed, I let me make myself a cup of tea and sit me down. I'd talk to myself until I had gained the strength to go back to taking care of God.

Taking care of God, however, kept getting harder. Instead of experiencing short periods of time when I couldn't sing or think, I would experience short periods of time when I could. It seemed that when all of me was present, exhaustion dominated. Most of the time I sat next to the bed, waiting until I felt strong enough to try again. To remain whole, I had to acknowledge my own needs. I couldn't spend every spare moment tending to God anymore. As a result, his progress toward health was slow at best. I was barely keeping God alive let alone fostering any hope for healing.

One day I was in my normal position, sitting by the bed, staring blankly into space, unable to sing or think. The next thing I knew, I was also sitting on the other side of the bed, giving myself a concerned look.

"This isn't getting you anywhere."

I looked up, mildly surprised. Then I considered the statement I had just made. "I know."

"What are you going to do now?"

"I'm not going to leave him, if that's what you wanted."

"Something needs to change."

I was right. Something *did* need to change.

I sat there in silence, thinking. Then I heard a knock at the door.

Another part of myself that I had rejected? I didn't bother getting up. "Come in."

It was a woman from our town with another large bag, presumably from my mother. She looked like she was almost afraid to encounter me, the one who left the town claiming that God was sick. She set the bag on the table and said, "God is so much bigger than this. He has a great plan for you. Even though things seem bad now, God will get better. I promise you that."

As I watched her walk out the door and back toward the town, I found comfort in what she had said. I clung to the thought that maybe she was right. Maybe the Man of God was right when he said God had great plans for me. Maybe this was part of them. I just needed to keep my chin up and stick it out. If I was committed to God no matter what, I would be rewarded. I repeated this as much as I was able. Some days it was easier to believe than others.

This began the era of what I like to call "mother's messengers." Every few days, someone from the town would come with a bag of food and some advice. I gave most of the food to God, but the advice was mine to cherish. Much of it was the same from one person to the next, and as it all blurred together, I became calloused and even more exhausted than I already was. Even so, I tried to remain hopeful. "Maybe the next person will be able to help us," I'd tell myself. "You never know . . . " Yes. Maybe.

"Have you taken the time to truly listen to God?" Another woman had made her way into the shelter. "It sounds like you've spent a lot of time listening to other people, but you haven't taken the time to truly tune in to what God might be saying to you."

She seemed nice enough, but I had nothing to offer her than my blunt hopelessness. I pointed toward the bed, "The only thing I hear from God is ragged breathing and a nasty cough now and then. What do you think he's trying to tell me?"

The woman left, defeated, but as soon as she walked out the door, I was sitting across from me at the table.

"How do you know she wasn't right?"

"How do you know she was?"

"That's not the point. Maybe you should try listening to God more."

I half-heartedly added it to my to-do list.

Another woman, full of joy and happiness, burst through my door with a huge smile on her face.

"Hello, friend! Do you know how much God loves you?"

I had nothing to give her but a heavy sigh. In response, she cheerily grabbed a chair and sat across from me.

"Listen," she said, "Once you realize how much God truly loves you, your life will change dramatically. God wants the best for your life. He wants you to live abundantly, and while that may be hard sometimes I promise you, his plans are bigger than anything you can imagine. It will all be worth it in the end." She gave me a huge smile as if she was expecting it to be contagious.

I tried desperately to smile with her. It was a futile attempt.

"Wait just a second, she may be right." I had split again and was standing behind the woman's chair.

"What do you mean she may be right?"

"Think about it. You've been trying so hard to take care of God, you haven't fully experienced his love. Let him take care of you for a change. Maybe he really does have plans for you if you'd just let him lead."

I gave myself a nasty look and purposefully directed my gaze to the bed, insinuating that God seemed incapable of leading at the moment.

I pretended not to see. "You should really be more open-minded. I thought you wanted to change."

"Okay, fine. I'll give it a try."

The woman was talking again, "Do you really love God? Do you want to follow him passionately with your whole self?"

"Yes!" I cried, because it was true. That was how I got myself into this situation in the first place. "Please, tell me what I need to do!"

"If you truly love God, you'll submit to him. Let him lead you. He loves you. He won't lead you astray."

The part of me behind the woman nodded vigorously. "See. I told you so."

After a little more talking, the woman wished me luck and left just as happily as she came in.

There I sat, alone with God, ready to submit. Then I realized I had no idea what that meant.

"Wait! How am I supposed to submit to God?"

The part of me that was standing beside the woman had taken her seat. "You heard what she said. Let him lead you."

I looked at myself incredulously. "You do realize that God is sick, right? He can't get up out of bed let alone lead me anywhere."

"Just try it."

"Okay." I sat there for awhile, trying to figure out the best way to "submit and let God lead." I filled my head with as many thoughts of God's love as possible, trying to think about all the great plans he might have in store for me, and where he might want to lead me. I made sure to open my mind to possibilities I couldn't even imagine. When I was ready, I turned to God all curled up on the bed, knelt next to him, and took his hand. "God, I want to submit my life to you. I want to follow where you lead. I want to live the way you want me to live."

He coughed a little. And nothing happened.

"It's hopeless!" I cried.

The part of me that had taken the happy woman's chair looked like I was thinking really hard. I tried to encourage myself, "Try harder!"

Over and over again, I tried to tell God that I wanted him to take control of my life. I asked him to help me. I begged and pleaded with him to show me the way. For hours, I sat there, in tears, willing God to do something, anything other than just lying there and waiting for me to tend to him.

Finally, I gave up and fell in an exhausted lump on the floor next to the bed. "Maybe this is where God wants me to be. Maybe I just need to keep taking care of him and that's all I can do for now. Maybe I just need to wait."

I turned to see what I thought of that idea and was immediately alarmed. A dark look had come into my eyes. "I know what's going on," I said quietly, with a touch of malice.

My breath caught. What was I thinking?

I stood up from my chair and pointed a finger at me, accusingly, "God's not sick! *You* are! You've been told what you need to do. So many people have come in to help you heal him and none of it has worked. Why hasn't it worked?" I took a step toward me. I could feel the tension in me growing and started backing away, afraid of what I might do.

"I don't know!" I sobbed, tears streaming down my face. I was so confused. I just wanted God to get better. I was trying my hardest.

"Don't lie to me. I can see right through you. Do you want to know why it's not working? I'll tell you." The raw cruelty that was beginning to surface made the hair on my neck stand on end. I kept trying to back up but realized I was now cornered between the wall and the bed. There was nowhere to go.

I looked at myself with a hatred I didn't know I possessed, "You don't want God to get better. You don't want to submit to him. It's easier for you to just tend to him and pretend to care. You'd rather he be sick."

"NO!" I cried, "I would never do a thing like that! I love him. You know that. How can you not know that?" I curled up in a ball on the floor and buried my head in my knees, hoping that this hateful accuser would go away.

Instead, I grabbed myself violently and threw me at the bed, "PROVE IT!" I screamed, "If you love God so much, then heal him!"

I could barely breathe I was crying so hard, and I couldn't think because of a throbbing in my head, but I was scared of what I might do if I didn't listen, scared that I might be right. Maybe I really was evil and self-centered. Maybe I really was the reason that God was sick and everyone had been right all along.

I reached out for God's hand and took it in mine, but no words would come out until I said weakly, "I can't."

The accuser had split and now there were two of them, hurling all sorts of verbal violence at me, "You're a failure! God will never get better and it's all because of you."

"You never actually loved God! You're just using him. You have ulterior motives."

As I knelt by the bed, holding God's hand, I could feel myself split again. Where part of me was too exhausted to respond, another part of me was crying in the corner. One accuser turned my attention to the crying me, while the other continued hurling abuse at the part of me holding God's hand.

"Stop crying! Do you think that will make me pity you? It's just a show. I know how you are. You're just going to try to manipulate me until I do what you want me to. I'm not going to fall for it!"

"You're pathetic! Look at you! You can't even stand on your own two feet. You can't fight me. You're just going to lay there and take everything I hurl at you aren't you? Well you know what? I hate you. I hate you with everything I have in me. I hate you because you are destroying God. You are evil."

And then the first blow came, and my world went black.

This whole time, I had been watching outside the window. I knew it was only a matter of time until I began to see the darkness within me. I had waited patiently, contained, and now I was finally able to watch it reveal itself to the parts of me that refused to admit its existence. What would I do now that I was confronted with it face to face?

A small smile began to form as I watched me hit myself over and over again. With every blow, I split into another set of me's. It was beautiful in its own perverse way, like a dance. I was amazed at the complexity within me, that I could even attempt this interaction. The pain coursed through me as well as the pleasure of having that much power. I could make myself writhe in pain. I was the only one who knew how to hurt me in the deepest way possible and then choose to do it.

I looked at the small, shriveled God on the bed and suppressed a laugh, remembering when a part of me believed that he would be able to save me. It wouldn't be long before the rest of me would realize what was going on, but until then, I would wait in my place, hiding outside the window.

Chapter 8

When I woke up, I couldn't tell whether or not my eyes were open. Everything was dark, I couldn't see a thing, and the throbbing in my head wouldn't go away. I tried to remember how I got here, but it was of no use. The last thing I could recall was the fight. I had been pushed up against the bed, holding God's hand, trying to heal him, but was unable to do it. Wait! Where was God? I tried to open my parched lips to call for him, tasting the blood in my mouth.

"He's not here," I said, a vicious sense of triumph echoing throughout the space.

I tried to turn toward the source of the voice, but sound was just as confusing as sight. It bounced off the walls before I had the chance to locate its origin.

"Who are you?" I barely managed to whisper the words.

"What a stupid question. I'm you. I'm everything you've refused to admit about yourself. I'm everything you're afraid of becoming. I'm here to tell you that there's no need to be afraid," I chuckled, "because you've become everything you're afraid of becoming. I'm right here."

I leaned in closer to my face so that I could see the two black holes that existed where my eyes should be, blacker than the darkness surrounding us.

In terror, I tried to back away.

"There's no use trying to get away from me. I'm part of you. You're stuck with me forever." I smiled, reveling in my fear, cherishing the power I finally gained, the attention I received after I had waited so long for recognition.

"No. No. This can't be," I said, curling myself into a ball, trying to shut out everything around me, but even as I closed my eyes, I was confronted with darkness. I couldn't get the image of the abyss behind my eyes out of my head.

"What are you going to do now that all the goodness is gone?" I asked. "Tell me, have you noticed your world getting darker and darker?"

I ignored my questions and countered with others, "Where am I? How did I get here?"

Amazed and amused at my blindness, I responded, "Why are you acting so disoriented? You brought yourself here."

"No. No, I wouldn't go here. I wouldn't choose to go here."

"You've been lying to yourself for too long. Don't forget. I'm just as much a part of you as you are. In fact, so are the rest of them."

Voices emerged out of the darkness. I could hear them yelling at each other, crying, accusing each other of all sorts of things. All of them were trying to convince themselves that they were good, pure, doing what was right, and yet the rage, enmity, and hopelessness that accompanied their words was stronger than what they were trying to prove.

My dark voice rang out above the chorus of voices, "You chose to come here. All of you chose to come here. You elected me to lead the way."

"No. I don't believe you." I put my hands over my ears, trying to block out the penetrating sound of my own voice.

I laughed again.

"You're evil," I whispered, trying to bury my head deeper in between my knees.

"I know." I leaned in closer to my covered ears, "And I'm you."

The cacophony of fighting voices escalated, echoing in the space until I could no longer make out what I was saying. I lost track of myself. One moment, I was the dark me, the next I was crying on the floor, the next I was attempting to comfort myself.

All of a sudden I started laughing at my feeble attempts to acknowledge my goodness. My head burst with the arguments. Every time I even tried to voice a thought, tried to fight something I had said earlier, I switched perspectives, challenging myself, "How do you know? Can you be certain? Or is that just what you want to think? Or what *they* want you to think? Why bother thinking at all?"

There were so many of me viciously pitted against each other that I felt as if I no longer had a voice. All that was left of me beyond the chaos was one long, agonizing scream.

Time stood still in the dark. I have no idea how many days I spent there being taunted by the dark part of me that had finally surfaced, accompanied by the chorus of arguing voices that made it impossible for me to think clearly. At first I made feeble attempts to fight back, but I was so weakened that I had no means with which to fight. I had spent so much time taking care of God that I had no idea how to interact with myself—especially my darker self. It seemed that the more exhausted I became, the louder the voices screamed at me and the stronger my darker self became.

"Look at you. Look at how perfectly wretched you are. You're so fragile. All they have to do is hurt God and you become helpless."

"Why did you let them do it anyway? How stupid are you that you just let them take advantage of you like that? Why didn't you stop them? Better yet: why did you give your heart to something so futile?"

A tear slipped down my cheek as I silently endured my words. They were questions that were all too familiar. I had tried to ignore them as I nursed God, but now as I sat in the dark, it was all I could think about. Why had I been so blind? Why did I think that God was strong when they abused him so easily? The only answer I could come up with was that there was something fundamentally wrong with me.

"You didn't give your heart to something futile," I countered. For a moment I became hopeful that I had come to my own rescue. "It's not God that's the problem. It's you! They never hurt God. They can't touch God. You just think God is sick, but it's not true. God loves you so much and wants the best for you and you just can't see it. You won't accept God's love. God would love you if only you would let him."

I felt as if my soul was being mangled. How was I unable to accept God's love when I loved him so deeply? Yet it must be true. God couldn't truly be sick. I was the problem. I must be too broken to be healed. I could never reach God. He would always be sick and silent to me, and I would never be able to heal him. I created my own hell because I couldn't feel God's love. And it was all my fault. In despair, I lamented the pain within me. If it hurt this much, why didn't it kill me? Why couldn't it just destroy me and be done?

I don't know how long the voices continued with their shoutings and rantings before I began to realize what was going on: This was all part of God's test to see if I truly loved him! If I just endured a little bit longer, God would come. He would save me. He'd tell me the truth about myself. I didn't have to believe any of these lies. That person that looked like a darker version of myself wasn't real just as God wasn't actually sick. This was God's way of helping me open myself up to his love. This was how I would learn to trust in him, even if I felt things weren't quite right. "Thank you God!" I cried even though I had assured myself earlier that he was nowhere to be seen. "I will be open to your love!"

When I heard this, I laughed. How could I be such a slow learner? When would I realize that God would never come?

"You're not real!" I yelled at my dark self. "I must be pure. I must be open to God's love. I will not doubt his strength!"

I shook my head, "Yeah, okay. Whatever you say."

Immediately I was pommeled with voices.

"You think you're so pure, but the truth is, you're a liar. You've been lying to yourself this whole time. You never really cared about God or about your town. You just wanted to make yourself feel good. You're corrupt. You'll never be able to do good because you'll never do it for the right reasons. You've lied to yourself about enough already. I bet you never really truly cared."

"NO!" I cried. "You're the liar. I am a good person! God has made me a good person! He's going to come and save me!"

I had turned myself into a fanatic and it wasn't working well. I watched the battle between the religious zealot and the dark side of me, each convinced they knew the truth. But as I sat there trying to discern what could possibly be real, I knew that I had no way of knowing the truth. I was a liar, and this darker side of myself proved it.

Now it was impossible for me to know whether I was telling the truth or hiding something from myself. Either the self-righteous part of me was intentionally blinding me to what was real or the dark part of me was skewing my vision, making me think that God was sick and that I was evil.

But if the dark part *was* me, wasn't I evil anyway? My head was beginning to get fuzzy. Perhaps the Man of God was right when he said I had sin in my life. Then again, did it matter any-more? I was outside our town walls, alone in the dark with no one but my wretched self for company.

"Why do you try anyway? You failed your town. You failed God. You've failed yourself. You're of no use to anyone. Why do you even exist?"

"It doesn't matter if I fail! God will win in the end! He will save me with his great love!"

And on it went.

The longer I stayed in the dark, the deeper I seemed to plunge into it. As a result, I became even better at hurting my-self. Soon I was able to render the religious zealot speechless as I uncovered the things that repulsed me the most and made them seem more real than anything else. I relished the power I found

within this new triumph. I knew how to hurt myself deeply—
and I enjoyed it. Every moment of it.

"Does it bother you that you're doing this to yourself?" I
would taunt, "Where do you think you learned all of this—how
to take the things you care about the most and use them to give
yourself the deepest pain? You like it, you know. You're secretly
enjoying it. That's why you're here. The townspeople hurt you
first and then you became addicted to the pain. When you left
them, you started doing it to yourself because you missed it. It
makes you feel alive. Why else did you come here? Why else
would you stay?"

I had nothing to say in response. How could I fight it? There
was no one here but me. Everything I said to myself I had come
up with alone, and I brought myself here alone. I truly was evil,
addicted to causing and enduring pain. How could I ever save
myself? I longed to cry out for help. I fantasized about someone
finding me and guiding me out of this place, but my hopes were
interrupted by more of my taunting.

"Is it that God can't save you or that he won't? Maybe God
prefers being sick to helping scum like you."

The only way to fight it was to sit and wait for God. And so
I did.

At last I crossed the line in my taunting. I crouched down
next to my helpless form and began to stroke my back sooth-
ingly as I wept, feeling alone, desolate and helpless. "It's so sad
isn't it?" I said. "So much pain. You can hardly bear it, can you?
Is it worth it? Do you really deserve this?"

I didn't answer, unable to stop the overflow of tears.

"You know the reason you're so fragile is these emotions.
The depth of your despair makes you vulnerable." I paused to let
myself wallow in my pain. "Stop caring. Stop caring about
everything. Become numb to the pain. And then," another
pause, "then, you can play with their emotions just like they
played with yours. It's been done to you, so you know the best
ways to do it. Think of the power you could gain. Think of how
fulfilling it would be to knowingly do to others what they did to

you and to benefit from it. Taste the triumph. Maybe all of this was worth it after all."

But I had gone too far. The idea I presented pushed against an immovable piece of my soul. I could listen to everything else because I knew it was somewhat true, but this, this was too much. I could no longer wait for God to save me. If he wouldn't come I'd have to do it myself. Energy coursed its way through my being and for the first time since I'd entered the dark, I dared to look into those dark holes as I stood to face myself.

"I refuse. That's not me," I said it so calmly, it took me off guard. This was not the religious zealot from earlier. This was deep, a part of myself that would not be shaken, even by the dark.

I was surprised by my sudden burst of inspiration. My darkness had held so much power for so long, I couldn't let go of it that easily. From the shadows, I fought back, "I suggested it. *You* suggested it."

"Listen." I said the word with an authority I didn't know I had, and for the first time since I entered the dark, I responded with silence. All of the voices in my head had stopped to listen, and in that moment I realized that all it took was a firm conviction, a belief held deeply enough that nothing else mattered. This was what I needed to confront myself, this deep knowing that there was something beyond myself that I could cling to. Despite all of the arguing voices in my head, I knew what I believed to be most dear, and it gave me the words I needed to hear.

I faced the dark holes in front of me with determination, "You've been confronting me with things I needed to see. You've been giving voice to things I've ignored—important things." I didn't break eye contact, "Thank you. I've needed this."

The dark me looked shocked.

"But, I cannot transcend my emotions. Just as you are a part of me, they are a part of me. To numb myself to them is to cease to be human. To use that numbness to abuse others is the opposite of who I am and we both know it."

For the first time, I didn't argue.

"I realize now that you are real, and it's important to listen to you, to be aware of you, because you're right. You're part of me." I paused. "But you're not all of me. And while you may have led me here, it's high time I led myself back out. I suggest you tag along."

And with that, I walked out of the dark as if I had known the entire time where I needed to go. The shelter sat before me, and I opened the door and rejoined God as he laid pathetically shriveled up on the bed just as I left him.

Chapter 9

The room was the same. God was the same. I had changed. I returned to the shelter with one phrase repeating itself in my head, "God never came."

I stared at him, lying on the bed, trying to figure out what to believe. I knew what people from my town would say. They'd say that God was testing me to see if I truly believed in him. They'd say I needed to endure despite everything. They'd continue to tell me that God was not really sick, that God loved me and this was part of his plan. I would learn so much if I just played along.

But I was lost in the darkest depths of myself, ready to die, prepared to destroy myself, crying out to God for deliverance. And God never came. The whole time he lay sick on this bed, shriveled up and dying. Did I believe in God anymore? He didn't seem worth believing in. Either God was utterly helpless or he was a traitor.

"Wait," a small pleading voice called out from next to the bed. I was back to sitting by God's side, holding his hand. "Can't you remember? Can't you remember when God was beautiful, when he loved you?"

Yes I remembered, but that's all it was. A memory. A haunting melody that distracted me from what was real. And that was

back before I had even encountered God in the first place. It was
a false memory at best.

"You could go back. You could keep tending to God," I said
as I dabbed sweat off his forehead with the cloth I always kept at
the end table. "He's still alive. That means there's hope he might
get better."

I shook my head. No, not after the betrayal I just experienced. I would not sacrifice myself for someone I didn't believe
in. Perhaps I would simply sit with God as he died.

"Please don't," I voiced quietly. "I love him. We've been
through so much together. I can't let him go." A tear slipped
down my cheek.

I was surprised by how weak this part of me had become.
Before, my need to cling to God and nurse him back to health
was the main force behind my existence. Now it was only a small
pleading voice. Even so, it held sway. I tried to reason with myself,

"Look, God is as good as dead. We all know that. Why can't
we just accept it?"

I immediately second-guessed my statement. I could feel
the tension within the room rising as I began to split again. My
head was spinning. For one faltering moment I had forgotten
that internal conflict was normal to me now. I couldn't think
without some part of me accusing me of having ulterior motives. I couldn't do anything without another part of me letting
me know that I should probably be doing something else. I had
said the wrong thing, and now just like so many times in the
dark, I found myself sitting, paralyzed by the silence with the
underlying threat of the many voices that could speak. Would I
always be afraid of myself?

Out of the silence, I heard my voice, disembodied, speak to
me in a strange, haunting way, "Be comforted. The source of
your pain will die today."

I didn't understand, nor did I have the clarity of mind to try.
Besides, I was becoming distracted by the rising temperature in
the room. God had started sweating a few minutes ago. I had

thought it was fever, but now I was beginning to feel the heat. It was oppressive. Almost as if it was calling me to leave the small shelter we had taken up residence in for . . . how long *was* that? I couldn't recall.

"I think the house is burning." I thought it might be a good idea to inform the group considering they were too busy thinking to notice.

They didn't respond.

"Hello? Don't you think it's getting hot in here?"

The smell of smoke was becoming more potent.

"Who set the house on fire?" I asked accusingly.

"Don't you think that's an irrelevant question? Don't you think we should be evacuating?"

"I guess, but still, somebody has to have done it. I'd like to know who."

"MOVE YOU NINCOMPOOPS! THE HOUSE IS ON FIRE!"

And with that the group started scrambling for the door.

"Wait! What about God?" I yelled.

"Leave him!" I responded. "What good is he anyway?"

"Are you kidding? I can't leave him!"

"Then grab him, but I'm getting out of here!"

I quickly went to the bed to get God. I have no idea where I got the strength to scoop God up and carry him out of the house. For once, it was good he was so frail.

I tried to run, from the burning house, from all of the different things people had told me, from the giant herd of me's trying to protect themselves from each other. With God in my arms, each step felt an inch closer to falling. Finally, even the small weight of God became too much to bear. I collapsed a few yards from the burning shelter, a symbol of what was left of me: chaos, fear, and a soul so scorched it would never stop burning. God had fallen to the ground with a groan and in my exhaustion I ended up strewn across his chest.

As I lay there, listening to God's barely discernible breathing, the crackling of the fire burning down any hope I had left, and the shouting voices from all the different parts of myself arguing, hitting each other, trying to figure out what to do, I felt a tear slip down my cheek. It all seemed utterly hopeless. I wanted to give up, but something had driven me this far. I loved God, but I knew this relationship would kill me if I kept trying to salvage it. By the looks of things God was about to die anyway.

I raised myself up off of God's chest and took his head in my hands, stroking his face, looking into his cold eyes, willing them to sparkle.

"God, please. Can't you remember? What has happened to you? Why can't you be the beautiful God they told me you were? Don't you know who you are?"

How could he know? I let the memories of his demise play in my mind. I watched as he was chained up, strangled, shoved around, thrown to the ground and left for dead. He had been through too much. Just like me, he had nothing left to give. Something that was once beautiful had faded into nothing, and now the two of us were left, empty shells, waiting.

I saw myself sitting on the ground, cradling God's head in my hands. The scene was tragic. The sky was dark, a blacker gray than I had ever seen, not very different from the rest of the landscape. As I looked around, I realized how long I must've been locked up in that shelter. I hadn't noticed the grass dry out and die, or the trees strip themselves naked. The fire I had started was the most lively thing in the landscape, almost as if it was livelier to die here than to be alive.

As I looked at myself holding God, I felt a surge of disgust. Why did I cling to him as if he was my only hope? Why did I want to preserve the life of someone who had been dying for months? It had only been a matter of time. Why couldn't I see that?

And who was this God that he was so well-loved? What had he done for me? He had been a part of my life for awhile, sure, but when I needed him most, he let others take advantage of him and left me at their mercy, striving to give my all to something that now seemed meaningless. I did everything for him and he gave me nothing but false hopes and dreams.

I turned around to see the rest of me, fighting over petty things like who was right and should I be emotional or not or would it be better for me to endure despite everything? I was paralyzed in this dead place, exhausted, blind, dying, destroying myself. And it was God's fault. He brought me here. He drained me. And as far as I could tell, God had no plan. He haunted me like a shadow, but he was never truly with me. He never truly cared about me. He was just taking what he could get. This whole time when I thought I had a friend, I was alone.

I could feel my breathing getting heavier and faster as I brooded on the wrongs done to me by this weak, pathetic God. It was time for me to do something drastic, something that might change my life, and I was ready. If this barren, burning wasteland was my life, I was ready for change. I had sunk so low, the worst thing I could do was to stay. This was hell. And it was time to leave.

I heard footsteps approaching. I turned around to see yet another vision of myself. I recognized the person in front of me: It was the dark me, everything I feared the most. My hair was unkempt and singed from the fire. Ashes covered my face. My clothes were in tatters. But beyond the messiness of it all, it was my eyes that brought me recognition. I remembered them from my time in the dark, blacker than night, as if beyond the irritated, red whites of my eyes, there were merely holes, windows into a darkness that threatened to consume me.

I was not afraid. I realized that this was the last part of me that I had turned away. This was the last part of me I had to let back into my life. This was the part that knew the whole time what needed to happen, but waited until I was ready. This was the source of the haunting voice that spoke to me in the shelter. When the time was right, I had struck the match. Yes, I had set the house on fire, and I was ready for more destruction. I was setting myself free. I was ready to do whatever it would take.

"Thought you might need this," I said, handing myself a dagger. I took it, staring in awe at the blisters decorating my arms. I caught myself staring. "Don't pity me," I said with a twisted smile. "I relish the pain. I will always be ready to embrace the darkness, and I have. Now it's your turn."

My hand closed around the handle of the dagger. I turned around, saw the two figures on the ground, breathed in everything around me, the chaos and anger, the memories of what got me to this place, the pain, the lies, but most of all, the truth that I needed to do this more than anything else. And I ran screaming toward the source of all my pain.

God was dying. His breathing was getting more and more labored. I couldn't comprehend what this meant. After all I had done, all the work I had put into helping him live just a day longer, just an hour longer—now I was striving for just a minute longer.

"God, please," I cried, a tear slipping down my cheek onto his face, "don't die. I need you here with me. I love you. I can't let you go."

And then, in a moment, my world changed for the second time. I heard a cry from behind me.

It pierced the air and rang in my ears until I thought my head would burst. The anguish and suffering in that cry was enough to tear my eyes from God's face for that one moment to see myself, in a rage sprinting toward us with a knife.

Before I realized what was happening, I cried out, "DON'T YOU EVER COME NEAR ME AGAIN!"

And the knife came from above and with a force stronger than I thought I had within me, I plunged it into God's chest and collapsed onto the ground beside myself.

When I saw myself with the knife, I was mesmerized. It seemed as if this had happened before, as if I had imagined it, fantasized about it, but had never acknowledged it.

And as the knife penetrated the heart of God, I felt a release.

For a few moments, I sat there in silence, staring at the knife thrust into the heart of the evil that threatened to destroy me, but also my closest friend. When I was ready, I turned to look upon God's lifeless face. He looked just the same. No expression, and an emptiness in his eyes. Had he been dead this whole time? Had he ever been alive?

Slowly, I let go of the dagger and turned to face myself. Reaching up, I took my face in my hands and looked into my eyes. I looked dazed, as if I couldn't register what had happened. "I'm sorry," I said, "It was time."

I turned back to gaze one last time at God's lifeless face. Closing my eyes, and letting my head drop, I let out a sigh, feeling a tainted hope, but hope nonetheless. "Thank you," I whispered.

And as I sat beside the corpse of God, I could embrace myself for the first time.

The Death

Chapter 10

I didn't bother to take the dagger. I had no interest in further violence, and it added a tragic flavor to the scene, a warning and a message of hope for anyone who might pass by: God is dead. He can't be used to hurt people anymore.

There was a heavy lightness in my step as I walked away. God was gone. I had nothing to worry about but myself. I had freed myself. Yet my best friend and companion was gone. And I was a murderer. I had killed the one I loved most in the world, and I just couldn't reconcile myself to it. Was it wrong for me to love him so deeply? Or should I not have killed him?

I felt old. My soul felt worn. The gravity of what I had done and what had driven me to do it settled upon me, and I could feel its weight on my shoulders. This was not a normal journey. The murder of God should have been a foreign concept to me. At this point, I could still recognize the strangeness of it, but the violence was not unexpected. By now I had watched enough violence to know that it was simply a part of life—whether or not it felt right.

As I began to dwell on it, I discovered that I didn't believe my act of murder was wrong. I had been lied to. The world I thought I lived in was drastically different than it seemed.

Oddly, I had to leave that world behind to see it clearly, and my murder of God was essential to that movement. Now I ventured forward with new eyes and tainted hope. Perhaps in this new world where God was dead I could find solace.

"Hey," I said gently, taking my hand in mine, "I'm here. I know it's impossible to replace God, but we've never really been able to exist together before. Now that God is gone, it's our turn. It's a bit of a change, but we can make it, and I'm glad we can truly walk together now, you know?"

It seemed to make sense. Maybe this wouldn't be so bad after all. By killing God, I had given myself the opportunity to get to know me. It was an interesting thought. How could it be that I had been living with myself my whole life, yet I still had so much to learn?

"So, where are we going anyway?" I asked.

I paused. Then suddenly, with great joy, I knew where I wanted to go. I knew that I could go there now that God was gone.

"Home," I said with a smile. "We're going home."

I walked by myself, hand in hand, closer and closer to the place I loved. With each step I noticed the grass beginning to perk up. I was starting to remember the color green, and the sky was no longer that dark, hopeless gray color. I could feel the energy flowing through me as I watched my world becoming alive again. Even within myself I could see the life coming back.

I was not at war anymore. Instead of arguing and accusing, I was conversing, cracking jokes, and simply enjoying what it meant to be me and to interact with myself. I remembered the things that made my soul sing and was finally able to experience them without the guilt of a dying God keeping me from joy.

I began to understand the deeper significance of what I had done. Before I gave myself that dagger, I had been paralyzed with indecision, not knowing if what I saw and felt was truly real or if I should continue to serve and love something everyone else told me was life-giving even if it killed me. I took a leap of faith when I killed God. I chose to trust myself. By killing God, I chose to let myself live.

After a few hours of journeying, to the side of the path, I saw a field of wildflowers, sitting there as if it had been waiting for me. I ran through it, twirling and dancing, collapsing amid all the different colors I had forgotten. What a relief! What joy! There was no tragic urgency. No sense of grave danger. Only an appreciation of what is.

"I don't have to do anything!" I exclaimed. I spent the next hour examining the intricate beauty of a small flower simply because I could. God was gone. I didn't have to take care of him. I didn't have to figure out what was wrong. I could simply experience the world and myself as we were. I had never realized that my world was so beautiful. When I left the field of flowers, a crown of daisies in my hair, I went skipping toward home in excited anticipation of what was to come.

Chapter 11

I knew that when I arrived at home, it would be different than when I left. I had been forced to leave because of the violence God and I had been experiencing, but I had been certain back then that it was all in my head. Now that God was gone, I assumed everything would be back to normal. But in my excitement, I had forgotten that God was the reason for the town's existence. The story of our town was that God had saved everyone. My story was that God almost killed me and I had to destroy him to save myself. Integrating the two stories would be impossible.

I felt a sense of foreboding as I reached the intimidating, yet unguarded town gate. Had I never noticed how gray and dismal the sky was here? Remembering the vibrant colors in the field of wildflowers, I hesitated for a moment, wondering if this was truly my home.

But if this wasn't home, then what was? This was where I had grown up, where I had learned to love. This was the beautiful place of my childhood. The violence that had driven me from it wasn't real. Or if it was, it was my fault. And I had taken care of it now. God was dead. Therefore, no one in the town could hurt him. Nor could they hurt me through him. I was ready to go back. It made sense to go back. Yes, I had to go back. This was home!

I reached for the handle of the massive door and pulled with all my might, the crown of daisies slipping off my head in the great effort it took to open it. A part of me observed it as payment for my entrance back into the town, but I suppressed the thought. I forced myself to smile. I was back. Everything was going to be okay.

I had hoped to slip in quietly, but it was not meant to be. By the time I reached my house, a whole crowd of family and friends had swarmed around me, pushing me toward the town square where my mother and her friends had hastily prepared a party complete with decorations and cake. Evidently she had been waiting for my return ever since I left.

"You're back!" they cried, smothering me in hugs and kisses.

I breathed a sigh of relief. It was truly all going to be okay. How wonderful it felt to be home.

Yet even as I was welcomed back into the town with great delight, I noticed changes. It seemed as if the town's population had doubled. For every two people I remembered, there were two more people I didn't. I was baffled by the sudden change. In all my years here, I had never experienced such a surge in the population. Then I looked closer at the crowd and found myself suppressing a gasp of horror as I realized what I was seeing. Everyone had a God.

"I thought I killed him," I mumbled to myself, eyes wide in confusion.

"You did," I replied.

"Then who are these Gods? Why are there so many of them? Why have I not noticed them before?"

For yet another moment in my life, I had no answers.

I was able to maintain a facade of happiness as everyone celebrated together. The people of the town outdid themselves in preparing cake and decorating the town square with balloons, streamers, and "Welcome Home" banners, so I didn't want to disappoint them by displaying my confusion. Rather than becoming upset at the new things I was seeing, I tried to analyze them.

As I encountered more and more people, I became fascinated by their Gods. Some looked exactly as mine had, but others were drastically different. While I had helped God stumble with me through the streets of our town, some people had hovering God companions floating in the air just above their heads. Other God companions were pulling their people on a leash in whatever direction the God chose. When the Man of God came to assure me how contented he was that I had "seen the light," I found myself staring in horror and amusement at the bobblehead God that followed him wherever he went, agreeing with everything he said.

No one else seemed to notice this dynamic. They all acted the same way they did before I left town. I began to worry about them. What if their Gods were like mine? I had to do something! They were being led astray just like I was! These people needed to be saved. They didn't deserve to go through the pain that I had experienced. No one did.

I could sense my anger boiling and knew it was dangerous to act too quickly. I called myself back to rational thought. "Wait. Does it matter?" I asked myself, "Do you remember what happened when people told you that your God was incorrect?"

I gasped, realizing what I could've done. Yes, of course I remembered. They beat God up. They made him sick—just like I wanted to do for these people. I furrowed my brow in confusion. Were the bullies I encountered before actually helping me, or were they the reason I had to kill God in the end? Perhaps they were both.

Yet I remembered the pain of seeing God torn apart. I couldn't imagine doing the same thing to the people of my town as had been done to me, and in truth, I had no desire to interact with their Gods.

"I think I'll just leave them alone," I decided.

But just as I concluded it would be better for me to say

nothing of my experiences outside our safe town walls, the celebrating crowds became silent, all eyes fixed on me.

"We want to know your story," the Man of God said. "Help us build our faith in God. Tell us of the evils beyond our town walls and how God saved you from them." I watched his bobble-head God nodding incessantly beside him as if encouraging me to speak.

I was shocked. The Man of God only wanted to keep the town exactly as it had been. It was now my job as the returned prodigal to convince everyone that going outside our town walls was the worst thing they could possibly do. I couldn't. In truth, venturing outside our town walls was the best thing I could have done.

I felt my heart beating faster and faster as I sat, mouth open in shock, paralyzed with fear. If I told them the truth, I would never belong here ever again. But if I lied, I would be hurting myself in an unforgivable way—especially after all I had experienced.

"I don't think you want to hear my story," I said finally after an extremely awkward stretch of silence. "God died." I took a deep breath, "and I came back because this is home." A tear slipped down my cheek as I said the word *home* because I knew the word was changing for me whether I wanted it to or not. I desperately hoped that I would be able to remain here anyway.

Immediately, people in the crowd began whispering, some talking to each other, some talking to their Gods. Detached, I watched their reactions in sullen silence. I had told them the truth in the simplest way I could. What happened next was not up to me.

The Man of God was first to act. He said nothing. He didn't even attempt to approach me. I surmised that trying to hurt me in the presence of so many townspeople would not be politically correct. Instead, he simply turned and walked away, his bobble-head God following him in agreement. It seemed he often turned his back when he didn't know how to respond. Perhaps it was safer that way.

The women from my weekly group who had mercilessly attacked God before I left the town clustered around me, but only to give me a few sentences from the Story and a pat on the shoulder. "This must be such a hard and trying time for you," said the new leader of the group. The pity in her voice separated us even further from one another. "Don't worry. God won't stay dead forever. He always comes back."

I didn't bother trying to explain to her that my tears were for the loss of my home, not the loss of my God. I didn't try to tell her that God didn't just die, I killed him. I didn't try to say how free I felt without him as I was walking back to the town, how the balloons, the cake and the celebratory decorations surrounding us spoke to me of my joy at the death of God rather than how he saved me and brought me home. No, God didn't bring me home. I brought myself home after a long, desperate struggle with a God who was supposed to save me. But I knew from the pity in her voice that if I tried to tell her, she wouldn't be able to hear me.

Soon, everyone had left. Some had given me other pieces of the Story as "encouragement." They didn't realize that the Story died for me when God did. Others simply left without acknowledging that anything had happened. I saw a few younger boys stealing extra pieces of cake to take back with them. I thought cynically to myself that within a few years, they'd be leaving the town "the right way," and within a few more years they'd come back "the right way" as well, with all sorts of stories to scare the general populace into remaining here for life.

As they left, I saw the younger girl with the weight in her stomach about to follow them, but she turned back to look at me as if trying to understand. I saw myself in her and couldn't help but wonder how many inappropriate questions she had asked in citizenship class that day. I tried to communicate to her without words. I wanted her to know that she was not alone, that her life would probably be difficult, but that maybe it would be worth it. I was interrupted as one of the boys took her hand and dragged her back with them. In that moment, I knew

I'd never see her again in the town. Perhaps many years later, we'd meet outside of it.

I sat for awhile in the town square, alone amid the reminders of the celebration that could have been. The remnants of the "Welcome back!" cake taunted me. It seemed sarcastic now along with the balloons and the colorful tablecloths that were turning gray like the sky above me.

"Is anyone going to celebrate with me?" I cried once I knew I was alone. "Why don't they understand that God was a tyrant who demanded everything from me and gave me nothing in return? Why can't they see how beautiful my life is now that God is dead?"

I felt lonelier and more depressed in the town than I had felt outside of it. What was the use of killing God if no one knew how to interact with me anymore?

Chapter 12

I left the bits of the Story I had been given next to the "Welcome back!" cake. I couldn't help but change the exclamation point to a question mark so that it now read, "Welcome back?" I deemed it more appropriate in my personal opinion, and I doubted anyone would notice it anyway.

I couldn't decide if I should stay in the town or head right back out the main gate. I still couldn't shake the idea that I would be leaving home, and despite everything, I couldn't stomach the thought of leaving. Where would I go? How could I leave everyone behind? What if the town needed the insights I gained through my experiences? Shouldn't I be helping the town instead of running away from it?

"Running away and leaving are two very different things," I heard a part of myself say. I stored away the grain of wisdom for the time being. I wanted to stay. I would give it a noble effort and if I felt absolutely desperate, perhaps then I would leave.

I walked to my parents' house, no longer knowing how they'd feel about my return. Thankfully they took me back, but I was regarded in cold silence. No one wanted to talk about what happened. My mother was hurt that her efforts at bringing me back had yielded unsatisfactory results, and both of them were embarrassed to be stuck with "the prodigal who hasn't actually returned." I couldn't blame them.

I got into a rhythm of hiding in my room and sneaking into our town gatherings a little bit after they started so that no one would need to talk to me. Now that God was dead, town meetings were almost disturbing. Whenever we sang to God, thanking him for everything he did for us, I watched each person within the town turn to their individual Gods and sing specifically to that God, sometimes drawing the God into an embrace when emotions ran especially high. The whole time, the Man of God sat up in the front with his bobble-head God, watching the proceedings and agreeing with whatever message the Man of God decided to convey.

"When did this place turn into such a circus?" I mumbled quietly to myself.

"An excellent question if I dare say so myself!" said someone behind me. I automatically assumed I was talking to myself again, but then I realized the voice was male.

I furrowed my brow and turned in the direction of the voice. Standing behind me was an interesting little man wearing a hat, very odd, round glasses, and carrying a black umbrella. Beyond his strange appearance, I was surprised and somewhat relieved to see that he had no God companion with him.

He gave me a reassuring smile and said, "Let's be honest with ourselves here, do we really want to be engaged in this— what word did you use? Circus? Or would it be more pleasant to take a stroll down the empty streets of town while everyone else is distracted with their personalized Gods?" It was becoming obvious that this man was not only aware of but delighted by my lack of God. Without thinking twice, I turned away from the special town meeting and went to roam the streets with this new and refreshing stranger.

"I assume you'd like to go straight this way?" he said, pointing straight at the town hall. I looked at him, trying to figure out if his question was supposed to be a sad attempt at humor, but for all I could tell he was completely serious. Starting to question the man's sanity, I remembered my own new role as village idiot.

"If we were interested in walking into a building, certainly, let's go that direction," I replied without a hint of sarcasm. "But weren't we planning on taking a stroll in the empty streets?" I asked innocently.

The man didn't seem a bit embarrassed. "Yes indeed, you are correct. I apologize, I seem to have a few more options than you do at the moment. Why don't you lead, if you don't mind."

"Not at all." I replied, suggesting to myself that perhaps this man was blind, giving good cause for his odd little glasses.

Twirling his umbrella nonchalantly, he fell in step with me.

"So tell me how a fine independent person such as yourself ended up in this town of God-followers. Are you an explorer or were you once one of them?"

Potential blindness and bad humor aside, this man was intriguing and unlike anyone I had ever met. For the first time I had run into a person who didn't speak of God with grave certainty and urgency. Instead, God was simply an interesting topic of conversation.

"I was one of them," I replied, a bit of my recent frustration leaking out into my tone.

"I see, I see! How fascinating! And how are you alone now? Did God leave you, or did you simply think away his existence?"

I looked at him curiously, debated whether or not to tell him the truth, and decided that he of all people would be okay with my story. "Neither. I killed him."

Obviously surprised, the man considered the concept, "You killed him." I could sense his respect for me was growing. "Hm. I've never heard that response before."

"Never heard that response before? Are these questions you ask the general populace on a regular basis?"

He seemed to be lost in thought but quickly snapped out of it. "Why, yes indeed. I'm making a study of it. I find gods to be quite fascinating things."

"Do continue," I prodded.

"For example, in this particular part of the world, it seems that people would say there is only one God and he has the attributes that they all agree on based on some fundamental Story or set of Rules. Does that seem right to you?"

"Yes," I said slowly, thinking about my new observations in contrast to what I once believed. "It's just that—" I stopped, not knowing how to explain myself.

"You've been seeing things differently since you . . . " he paused, still playing with the concept in his mind, "killed God?"

"Yes!" I replied, excited that someone finally understood. I burst into explanation, "Everyone has a God! I have no idea where they all come from, and while they look similar, they're all a bit different—almost as if they're personalized companions."

"Fascinating isn't it? The belief is radically different from the reality. Would make anyone want to study this 'God' phenomenon, don't you think?"

I nodded in agreement, still trying to process this new way of thinking.

He continued on with his line of thought, "Of course everything gets more complicated once you take in the Glasses Variable."

"The Glasses Variable?"

"Why yes," he turned to look at me directly, "I suppose you can see my glasses?"

"Of course I can see your glasses. You're wearing them."

"May I ask you a question then? Would you say your glasses are similar to mine or different?"

"What are you talking about? I don't wear glasses."

He grinned, "Thought you'd say that."

I looked at him incredulously, "You're not implying that I'm wearing glasses and am unaware of the fact, are you? Because that's simply ridiculous."

"Yes, in fact, I am!" His grin broke out into a full smile. I could tell he'd had this conversation before and we were getting to his favorite part.

"I am not!" I argued, lifting up my hands to my face to rub my eyes in proof that there was nothing stopping me from doing it. But as I went to touch my hands to my face, I felt something hard. "What?" I cried, "This is impossible!"

He continued smiling, knowing what I was about to try next.

I reached to the side of my face to lift them off, but to no avail. They wouldn't move. "What? I'm wearing invisible, immovable glasses?"

"Evidently so."

I couldn't believe it! How was it possible that I had spent all this time wearing glasses and completely unaware of it? "Does this mean other people are wearing glasses as well?"

"From my experience, yes. Everyone wears glasses."

"Then why have I only been able to see your glasses and not other people's?" I asked, trying to understand.

"It's a common phenomenon when I'm in this part of the world that people see my glasses. I'm so different from them they can't help but notice. I see the world differently than they do."

"So in your homeland, people don't notice your glasses?"

"It's hard to say. My native land is very aware of the Glasses Variable. That's how I came to know about it. From my experience, once you become aware of the Glasses Variable, you become aware of everyone's glasses whether they see like you do or not." He paused a moment to allow me to process.

"Okay, so everyone's wearing glasses, and now that you've informed me of this, I'm probably going to see glasses on everyone I meet. But why does it matter? Who cares if we're all wearing glasses?"

"Well, it goes back to my original question. Would you say your glasses are similar to mine or different?"

"I have no idea. I haven't seen my glasses. Apparently I can't take them off."

"Yes, but you've seen through them. I can tell you right now that we're both wearing very different glasses. I bet if you think through our interactions you can too."

Immediately, I recalled what he was referring to. I grinned and used his tone of voice, "Tell me friend, are we walking on a street right now?"

Delighted, he responded, "Why, no. We most certainly are not!"

I shook my head in amazement. "Wait. How do I know you're not just saying that?"

He smirked. "You don't. But think it through. Surely before now you've noticed other townspeople using a different route than you to approach the same destination?"

I thought for a moment. While I had never acknowledged it before, I could recall countless times when people had taken a different route than me to get somewhere in the town. Some times, I even found their routes silly because I saw them walking in circles to avoid using streets that were perfectly functional. "Yes, actually I have noticed. I just always thought that they had stopped off somewhere on an errand or were trying to get more exercise. I didn't realize. . . . "

"They might be avoiding an obstacle you can't see?"

I nodded. Things were beginning to make sense. "So, does this mean that the Gods I see everyone interacting with may or may not be what someone else sees?"

"Precisely."

"Then how am I supposed to know what's real? How can I possibly tell if what I see is legitimate?"

He stroked his beard, thinking. "I guess it's a matter of faith. And besides that, what other choice do you have?"

I was frustrated. My world had just gotten much more complicated. I started to pine after the times when all I had to worry about was my dying God.

"And actually," he began again, interrupting my thoughts, "when you think things through, there are plenty more things we all see than things we disagree on."

"Hmph," I pretended to listen. I was still trying to figure out the truth about all of the gods I had seen. Were they real? Were they destructive like mine was? Could I ask someone about their relationship with God and get an understandable answer? Or would they blame all their problems on themselves like I was prone to do? How could I possibly know anything for certain? My head was starting to hurt. I let out a cry of exasperation, "How can we communicate with each other if we don't see things the same way?"

He responded smoothly, as if my emotional outburst had no effect on him, "A valid question. Though, it seems that we *do* communicate somehow, doesn't it?"

I looked at him, calculating. It was true. I had lived my life completely unaware of this Glasses Variable until now. From what I could recall, the people in my life had communicated with me somewhat decently. And if I couldn't effectively communicate with this man, we wouldn't be having this conversation. Perhaps it wasn't as complicated as I thought.

He continued, "Many people who become aware of the Glasses Variable simply gather as much information as they can about how another person sees things and then translate their view into a language the other person can understand through that individual's unique glasses."

"How exhausting!" I had no intention of doing anything of the sort.

"You'd be surprised how quickly it becomes second nature. Some people treat it like a game." He shrugged. "Most of the time, though, I think we unknowingly lose things in translation from one pair of glasses to the next. In reality, we can only expect to get faint glimmers of how people actually see things."

In reality! How could he say that after all this nonsense about a Glasses Variable? "This means that I probably see a very different world than you do, then," I surmised.

"Indeed it does," and as he said this, he very calmly opened his umbrella and began walking underneath it as if it made perfect sense to do so.

"Now wait just one second. Why did you do that?"

He looked at me with another of his grins, "It's raining." I could hear the implied "obviously" in his tone.

This was becoming too much. "Okay, the glasses thing I get, but rain has nothing to do with whether you can see it or not and everything to do with whether or not you're getting wet."

"I know."

"It's *not* raining."

"This is true . . . where you are, but not necessarily in my case."

"What can you possibly mean by that statement?"

"Nothing, other than that we're living in different worlds."

"Hold on! We're talking to each other. We're walking down . . . " I tried to think of the right way to put it, "*my* street together."

"That's the miracle, it would seem. How is it possible that we are interacting when we live in different worlds?"

"Well, I don't think we are living in different worlds."

"Tell me, has anyone ever told you something with great certainty and you knew he couldn't possibly be right, yet he wouldn't back down?"

Suddenly I realized that this strange man with glasses was making sense of a lot of my experiences. I remembered myself desperately asking everyone about God's cough, hoping that someone could explain to me what was going on, or at least help me heal him. Then I remembered the Man of God saying so assuredly, "I'm not strangling God," as I saw him holding God in a locked grip.

"Yes!" I said. "Yes I have."

He nodded with satisfaction. Then gently, he asked, "Out of curiosity, how did you respond?"

I felt the old pain wash over me. Immediately my voice dropped, betraying the great sadness I carried with me, "I assumed that person was right and that I was crazy or that there was something wrong with me."

Again, he nodded, this time with empathy. "It happens a lot." He paused. "That's why you don't have your God anymore, isn't it?"

I sighed, "Yeah. You could say that."

For a moment, we walked in silence. The man was giving me a chance to remember, to relive, to realize that my past was past so that I could allow myself to reenter the present. When I was ready, I broke the silence. "So, do you have any idea why we can be having this conversation right now when we are wearing different glasses and living in different worlds?" I asked, beginning to feel fragile and alone.

He looked at me, humility in his eyes. "Somehow our worlds have collided." He paused to search my eyes for a moment, as if he was trying to see just beyond them. I felt vulnerable, but I didn't break his gaze. Finally, when I thought I could no longer bear his scrutiny, he shifted it to the street ahead and continued, "Because of our meeting, we will leave one another with changed perspectives. Traces of your world have entered mine and traces of my world have entered yours."

I felt desolate. "How can this be? How can we exist in such a way? How can we manage to survive on our own?"

"It's amazing to ponder isn't it?" He looked longingly off into the distance. "It seems that we do, in fact, exist in such a way, and we have survived, living in our colliding worlds. What I have sensed within my exploration is that there is more than just our small universes. We are part of something larger that allows our worlds to collide." He sighed. "That's why I've taken up the study of gods. I think we know that there's something out there that's beyond us, something that we all know yet can't describe or fully understand, something real."

Something *real*. The word touched a deep longing in me. How I longed for something real, something trustworthy and unchanging, something that defied my world, that interrupted it with its realness. I didn't want to be alone.

"I think we're afraid of it," he continued, "yet we long for it, deeply. I think, maybe, that's what all this god business is about. But these caricatures that I keep seeing people traveling with, they are so small. Most peoples' gods look human just like they are. How arrogant, to assume that God looks like us." He shook his head half in disgust, half in wonder.

I noticed that my breathing had deepened, as if I was trying to take in as much as I could from this collision of our worlds, "And what now?" I asked, "Why is being aware of this vastness worth the energy it takes to attempt to understand it?"

I knew this question had resonated with something deep inside him. He said his next words with such certainty and purpose, I could not help but give him my full attention.

"In all of my searching, observing, colliding, I have learned two things: First, things are the way they are for profoundly sound reasons. I may never understand, but I can always trust this to be true. Second, it is most important, though virtually impossible, to try to discover and experience what is."

He closed his eyes, as if seeing a memory play through his mind, then continued, "I have heard of so many 'supposed to's.'" He shook his head, as if trying to shake them out of his memory. "They get in the way. They are simply a part of our personal worlds that we create. They isolate us from one another. When I take the time and energy to fully immerse myself in what is, I can sense that our worlds are constantly moving, constantly changing. We spend so much time colliding with each other. There must be a rhythm to it. Is it not possible that some day, if we allow this movement to continue simply as it is without trying desperately to turn it into what it's 'supposed to be' according to our glasses and our individual worlds, that maybe our isolated worlds will be joined? Is it not possible that we might all become one and experience the wholeness that we long for?"

I had no answer for him but the sense of wonder and gratitude that was arising in me. There were no words for it, but he acknowledged it with a nod.

"You didn't fit in, did you?" I asked him. "Your native land where they're aware of the Glasses Variable, they don't believe in this stuff about a bigger world or becoming whole, do they?"

He smiled and winked at me. "The ones who don't fit in, go exploring, it would seem."

The ones who don't fit in go exploring.

The phrase stuck with me, taunting me in a playful way as I considered the full implications of what it meant. The conversation I had with the Man with Glasses had changed my world completely. While before, I felt compelled to stay in the place I once called home and force myself to fit in, I now felt as if I might want to try something completely different . . . and it would be okay.

There's a big difference between running away and leaving.

My own words came back to me, but this time they made me ponder what the man had said. Something *real*. I wanted to find it. I wanted to experience what is. This town was limiting to me now. I wanted to find something that was everyone's, something that interrupted my life and the lives of all of us whether or not we lived within the town's walls. I was ready. It was time to leave so I could start exploring.

In that moment, I looked ahead in hope. Suddenly I saw through my glasses how my world had changed. Instead of a town full of buildings and streets with one massive wall to protect it, we were standing on a forked path at the edge of a small village surrounded by a tiny little fence, barely noticeable. For the moment, my town was no longer intimidating, nor did it mandate which direction I needed to walk. It simply existed as it was. It was no longer something to run away from, simply something to leave to search for other things. I looked at the forked path before me. Immediately, I sensed that one path was for me, the other for the Man with Glasses.

"It looks like it's time to for us to go our separate ways, then," I said.

"So it would seem," the Man with Glasses gave me a meaningful look that I didn't fully understand. "This has been very refreshing for me. I hope that one day we will meet again and you can tell me what happens after the death of your god."

"I hope so too."

I watched as he took the right side of the fork. It wasn't until I reached the now tiny town gate that I fully realized the evidence of our colliding worlds. Reassured, I approached it and lifted the latch. Slowly, tentatively, I pushed open the gate and slipped through. I took one step away from what I once called home. And then another. And then another. Soon, I looked just as the Man with Glasses would have looked to me. I was traveling with certainty to nowhere.

Around midday, I found myself in front of another large wall.

"Hello?" I called out, curious as to why another town existed in such close proximity to mine.

There was no answer.

Perhaps it was better this way. I didn't know what kind of a town was inside those walls. Nor was I truly interested in finding a town. I was just about to walk away, when the door opened and I saw two travelers, a man and a woman emerge. The woman was obviously pregnant. Both of them were accompanied by God companions.

"Did you want in?" the woman asked kindly, holding the door.

"I don't know," I answered. I was taken off guard by the combination of having a healthy God companion and leaving a town. It didn't make sense to me. "May I ask why you're leaving?"

"Oh, it's simple, really. It's just that we're expecting." She rubbed her swelling belly in the way pregnant mothers do. "Our town didn't have very many children. We're hoping to move to another town that's more family oriented."

"I've never heard of moving from one town to another before," I said.

"Really?" she seemed surprised by my ignorance. "There's a whole network of towns here. It's amazing the big family we have, all of us saved by God and protected by him."

I was even more confused. "I was told it was dangerous outside our town walls."

This time the man piped up, "It is, figuratively speaking. What people are really saying is that it's dangerous to live outside of a town, but to move from one town to another, that's perfectly safe. What's important is to stay in the land of God-followers."

Now I was getting somewhere. "So, how do you get out of the land of God-followers?" I asked. "Figuratively speaking, of course," I added so as not to alarm them.

The man looked at me suspiciously anyway. "I'm not really sure. All I know is that these paths lead along the network of towns. If you're on a path, you'll find a town. Don't stray from the path and you'll have nothing to worry about."

"Good to know." I surveyed the off-path terrain and decided that it looked walkable. "Listen, thanks so much for your help."

"No problem," the woman said.

The man was still eyeing me suspiciously. "Did you want in, then?" he asked.

"No, thank you." I replied and cheerfully began walking off the path. "It was great to meet you," I called out behind me. "I hope you find a suitable town." I didn't bother to turn around to see the shocked looks on their faces.

Chapter 13

"It hurts," I said quietly.

"What?" I was confused. This was unexpected. It had been a few days since I left the path and I had been enjoying myself immensely. Even though I had left the path, I kept running into paths. Because I had no map and limited experience outside of my own town, I decided not to let it bother me unless I recognized something from before. As long as I never stayed on a path, I'd eventually find my way out of the land of God-followers.

Naturally, I looked very strange to other travelers on the paths, since I was traveling on no path at all in the wrong direction. This brought on quite a few interesting conversations. There were a few different types of travelers. Many were just like the young couple I met, simply looking for a town with a few differences from their original home. Others had had painful experiences like I did, but they had not been driven to kill their Gods. Instead, they looked to their Gods to help them decide which town they'd go to next. Still others were people sent especially from the towns to find people like me and convince them to come back.

I would've been scared of these individuals had I not been godless. Now, I simply tried to introduce them to the Glasses Variable. Some people understood, some people didn't understand at all. Other people were so terrified by the idea that they started looking for the God who had inspired such a concept so they could do away with him. I would just smile to myself in those times, knowing there was nothing they could do to hurt me because God was dead.

Overall, I was having a marvelous time outside my town's walls. I was exploring, on a quest to find the things that remained the same within my world and everyone else's, evidence of something Real. I had new purpose and direction. I was traveling to a land beyond the God-followers. Life was looking up. So how could I possibly be in pain?

"I can't make it stop. I've been trying to make it stop, but it won't go away."

I could hear the fragility in my voice, the panic. Something was definitely wrong.

"Here," I said motioning to a nearby tree. "Why don't you sit down and rest for a little bit."

I didn't argue. I couldn't describe the pain I felt. It was too deep and completely unreachable. My powerlessness made it worse as I sat and rocked myself back and forth, futilely trying to make it go away.

I sat down beside me and tried to console myself while at the same time trying to coax out an explanation of the problem. "Do you have any idea what started it?"

"I can't remember. It's been here for a while." Tears began to stream down my face.

I knew. I hadn't wanted to admit it, but I knew. The haunting melody of the dead God I left behind had been tormenting me since I left him with the dagger through his heart, but I was too distracted leaving the town to acknowledge it, too distracted to stop it from getting inside of me and singing to my soul, slowly reminding me of how I got here, penetrating layer through layer of protection until it reached the deepest part of who I was. The wound there was deep, and I knew the sickening melody of my dead God hadn't caused it. It simply opened it up and laid it bare in front of me, forcing me to experience its pain.

"When did this happen?" I didn't expect an answer. I was simply confused. No one had plunged a dagger into my heart. No one had thrown me to the ground and beaten me up. All of those horrible things were done to God. I had hardened as I had learned that God was not worth the care it took to keep him alive amid the abuse, but that had nothing to do with me now. I had learned not to love God anymore. Why did it hurt so much that he was dead?

I could no longer console myself. I had become another victim of my wound. The waves of pain were overtaking me. I needed help, but my God was dead, and I had no idea where I was. My mind became blank, my eyes empty, and my world was slowly turning into a sea of mist.

With a start, I realized how vulnerable I was. I needed to get somewhere safe. I didn't want anyone to find me. They would try to make me better by shoving a new God into my life, and I was too weak to survive being used again. I had seen their Gods. They looked just like mine. I could not relive the same story. If it happened again while I was in this state, it would kill me.

I began to split again. The many different parts of me emerged; soon there was a semicircle surrounding the tree where I sat with my deeply wounded self, trying to figure out how to heal. The discussion was urgent and energized. I had to figure out the best way to hide my vulnerability from those who might seek to harm it. Arrangements were made, instructions were given, and I watched as each part of me willingly accepted its role in the new system of defense I was creating. Amazed at this new sense of protectiveness, I realized that I was finally beginning to care about myself. Even though God was dead, I could feel loved. Even if I was all I had left, I knew that I was in my own caring hands. Perhaps being alone wasn't as devastating as it seemed.

By the time I was done, a bodyguard had been created. When I got up from my place at the tree, I was surrounded by different parts of myself, stationed to protect the weakened part of me in the middle. I traveled on in a pack, and for some time I was safe.

There was one fundamental flaw in my beautifully orchestrated defense: I had no means with which to protect me from myself.

It wasn't long before the wound was festering.

I don't know how it happened, but within a few days, part of me had become convinced that God had resurrected himself and was healthy. I just needed to return to the town to find him. Every day, I would say to myself, "Maybe we should return to the town and try to get God to come back. We've spent enough time without him now. It would be better if he were here. It would be better to go home."

Even so, enough of me knew that my deepest self was needed to look for God, and it was far too wounded to put forth the energy it would take to even begin the search. "No." I'd say, "Not yet. I haven't healed. I can't look for God."

And so I'd let the matter drop. But each day the same conversation would occur.

"Are you ready to find God yet?"

"No. It's not time."

After many days of asking and many days of answering "no, it's not time," my darker self, irritated and tired of this fruitless pattern, forced its way into the conversation.

"You realize you can't go back, right? He's dead. He'll always be dead." I sounded bored.

The fact that my darker self had spoken made me want to fight back. "But in the Story, they talk about God resurrecting, right? It makes perfect sense that he would rise from the dead." It was worth a try, but it was an empty argument. When I killed God, the Story died too.

I rolled my eyes. Would I always be so stubbornly idiotic?

"Listen. You killed him. *You* did. You wanted to. You *needed* to. Do you really want him back?"

"Just think of the story I could tell everyone. I'd be able to go home!" I began to daydream of the past when God wasn't sick or dead and I actually belonged in my town. Maybe if I truly believed, everything would be okay again.

I was exasperated. I knew what was going on. I didn't really want God to come back. I didn't want to return to the town either. I just wanted the pain to go away. "It took forever for you to get the nerve up to kill him, and now you won't let him die? Just let it rest. Move on. You can only go forward."

Why was it that the dark in me spoke more truth than the rest? I didn't understand, but my advice was sound.

I knew that I was trapped in my own world, and I didn't like it. The mist was growing. Soon I couldn't see anything around me. People would often appear directly in front of me and I couldn't see them until the last moment. The bodyguard became more and more defensive as a result. It wasn't long until I began to live in a loud silence, presenting the coldest, strongest, most distant parts of myself to the travelers I met.

Meeting people, exploring, was of no interest to me anymore. I had forgotten about my quest to find something Real. I was deeply hurt and it was getting worse. I couldn't heal myself, but I couldn't let anyone else in. All of my energy was needed to survive.

"If God was here, I wouldn't have to think about this wound. I could spend all my time taking care of him." I yearned for God. At least I knew what I was doing when he was draining me of all my energy. At least when I was destroying myself, I felt like I had purpose. Now I was alone and empty of everything except my need to stay alive, and even that was starting to seem pointless.

"You were about to die. It wouldn't be any different if God was here now." I was still bored with the whole situation. It was the same old story. This was exactly what happened with God. He got sick and life was hell until I killed him. If there was a part of me that was deeply wounded, why didn't I just kill it too and put it out of its misery? It was better than trying to stop the pain by regressing. The bodyguard I had created was formed by the strong part of me. Why didn't I just keep those parts instead of centering around this vulnerable, sickly mess? Survival of the fittest. It made much more sense than this constant care and worry.

"Where are you trying to go so fast that you insist on being destructively efficient?" I asked my darker self, an amusement ringing out within my calming presence.

I didn't have an answer. I was annoyed. It was this calm presence that had given me the strength to leave the dark, back before I killed God.

"Pain is a gift if it is acknowledged properly," I continued. "It needs to be listened to, not avoided."

I gave myself an insolent glare.

I responded with a wry, knowing smile, "You know this as well as anyone."

"Hmph."

"It's time to stop."

I groaned. I didn't want to stop. I didn't care if I needed to.

But the rest of me listened intently, and I started nodding in agreement. There was nothing more I could do except get myself into trouble. Stopping seemed to be the best option I had left.

I sat down, letting my wounded self rest against a tree as the bodyguard sat around me at attention. Strangely, I recognized the tree I was leaning against. It was the same one I had stopped at back when I created the bodyguard. Weakly, I acknowledged that for all the wandering I had done, I had gotten nowhere. I was lost. I was sick. I was alone. And I no longer had the strength to care.

I sat there alone for a while. A part of me started to look for the parallels between this situation and the time when God was sick. It was a fascinating exercise. Where before I had completely ignored myself to tend to the injured God, now *I* was the sick one and the only way to tend to myself was to stop trying so hard so that I *could* pay attention to me.

It was difficult at first. If the pain hadn't kept me from being able to do anything, I wouldn't have been able to stay still. Despite my weak state there was a strong drive within me. I needed to survive. I had to heal. It made more sense to me that I should be doing something to make that happen, but nothing worked, and the sage within me had told me to stop. So I sat.

I started to fantasize about being found. Maybe the Man with Glasses would discover me and somehow get me to a safe place. He was an explorer, so he should know the area, right? Maybe he'd even take me to his native land. I'd probably find more solace there than in this place of God-followers.

What would he say if he saw me? Perhaps I wouldn't even look wounded to him. The Glasses Variable was so frustrating. That familiar questions plagued me again: How could I be certain of anything? Was I truly sick? Would I ever know?

Yet these were the same questions I had asked about God not so long ago. Was God truly sick? Or was I just seeing things? I wanted to cry out in frustration! There was no way of knowing anything!

The mist was getting thicker and thicker. It was so thick now that I debated whether it was truly a tree I was leaning against or the mist itself. After all, how was I to know what was real and what was not? I had no license to decide that. No one did.

I had almost convinced myself that it was in fact, a very solid patch of mist behind me when I heard a voice call out, "Hey! Are you alright?"

A plethora of emotions rushed through me. Relief that I would not be stuck here forever. Gratitude that perhaps I would not be confused and in pain any longer. But after these feelings came fear. I had been discovered, and I was weak. So many horrible things could happen if I didn't stay on guard.

I could tell the voice belonged to a woman, but that was all. I couldn't see. I didn't know how close she was or whether or not she had a god with her. I didn't know what to do. Could I trust her with my wounded self? Should I respond?

Her glasses were the first thing I saw. It dawned on me that she could probably see just fine. It was only my personal world that was shrouded in blinding mist. Though I didn't want to admit it, I was powerless to defend myself. It was solely because of this that I decided to tell the truth.

"No." I was not all right. *No.* One simple word with so much meaning. I could've tried to convince her to be on her way, but I had told the truth. Now I would be stuck with the consequences.

She walked right through the bodyguard and approached my wounded self. I took note that she must have powerful glasses. She knelt down and looked at me with compassion in her eyes. "You're hurt." She said it in a way that seemed truthful. It wasn't, "Your God is gone" or "There's something wrong with you." It was simply "You're hurt." It was gentle. It was what I needed to hear. It allowed me to see myself in a new way. I could watch my story without blaming myself for everything that had happened, and it was okay that I was in pain because I was hurt. And now I was stuck at the foot of this tree, trapped in my world of mist and uncertainty, feeling the pain I had carried with me since before I even began trying to heal God.

"Yes," I whispered, "Please help me." I took a deep breath and my eyelids fluttered with the sleep they had been craving. I let them close. I had gotten myself where I needed to be. Now I could rest.

Chapter 14

I woke up feeling safer than I had since the first time I heard God's cough. The bodyguard was gone. More accurately, the bodyguard had merged with the rest of me. Yet even with this merging, my woundedness was what surfaced, evidence that I was sicker than I thought. I noted that while I knew I was wounded before, I had been too busy trying to survive to actually experience it. I had only known cognitively that something was wrong. Moments of pain had been scattered throughout my efforts to keep myself safe, but they never lasted long enough for me to fully acknowledge my state of being. Now I had finally been given the opportunity.

I could no longer feel any connection to my body. It was as if the only thing left of me was my consciousness—and even that was questionable. I tried to take in my surroundings but could only see blurred colors. The more I tried to focus, the more the colors split and scattered, furthering my disorientation.

My mind was in disarray. I didn't know what was real. I hadn't been ready for the thoughts and concepts the Man with Glasses revealed to me. I had just killed God and lost my home, the only things I could cling to for certainty and solid footing.

Now I had nothing. I could believe or disbelieve anything because I had no idea where I stood. A small pang of regret appeared in my vision, a swirl of mournful purple combining with other blurs of color that meant nothing and everything all at once. I wished I could go back. Wouldn't it have been easier to cling to God until I died than to have to live knowing that I had killed him and that things could never go back to the way they were?

Faith.

The word barged into my world, an intruder, walking amid the colorful blurs as if to say, "I'm still here. Have you forgotten?"

I recalled claiming my murder of God as an act of faith. Faith in what? That was the question. Even so, it made me think that perhaps all this was worth it. I had chosen a difficult journey, but my suffering might not be in vain.

It was time to listen to my pain. I tried to get back in touch with my body. First I told my eyes to shut so the blurs of color would stop tormenting me. I was surprised how quickly they obeyed. I squeezed them tightly shut and opened them again. Then I repeated the action until I had recovered awareness of my head.

Immediately, I regretted it. Searing pain ripped through my brain as if someone had driven a knife from above one ear to the other. Now that I was whole again, I was finally experiencing the cuts I had made to split one part of me from another. And those cuts were many. Even so, I knew that this was the only way for me to regain myself.

Terrified, I pushed through the pain and forced myself to continue. I told my lungs to breathe. *In. Out. In. Out.* I coached them, retaught them what it meant to be alive. Slowly, I managed to regain awareness of my chest, but not without further cost. I felt limited, as if I could only breathe so deeply without another knife splitting me in half. I began with short, shallow breaths, but determinedly, I insisted that I breathe more deeply. I told myself it was okay to cry out as long as I kept going deeper.

I managed to push the air down further and further until I reached the deepest part of who I was. My breathing became deep and would have been relaxed had I not been fighting pain every time I took a breath.

It was then that I discovered the previous pains to be mere surface wounds. The wound inside of me was much more severe, crippling, and unreachable. Strangely, it didn't give me the urge to cry out in agony as much as it did to give up completely, to turn back around and retreat to my world of blurred colors rather than face this powerlessness, this vulnerability.

As if on cue, the haunting melody began whispering to that deep wound, aggravating it. I could not take much more awareness. I chose to stare at the ceiling, trying to channel all my pain into an attempt to drill a hole through it, a potential escape.

I laid there, waiting for it to stop. I started to recall other moments of suffering I had experienced: holding God and weeping as the Man of God left us, crying out as I watched God being abused by people in the town. Then I remembered the suffering I had experienced in the dark as I had railed at myself, accusing myself of doing things that hurt me deeply. Strangely, the pain I was experiencing now was refreshing in comparison to the dark. It made me feel real, as if I was part of something larger than myself, as if the pain I was experiencing now was making me whole.

When I reached the point of ultimate desperation, about to give up, willing myself back to unconsciousness, I felt a shifting within me, and the room refocused. The pain was no longer unbearable, although it didn't entirely vanish. It occurred to me that I had just done a significant task. I had allowed myself to experience my own pure pain for the first time.

Now I could see that I was in a bed in a small room. There was a small table next to the bed with a chair beside it. While I felt safe, I reminded myself not to be naive. It was good that I had been able to go through that time of self-realization, but it didn't mean I no longer needed to be on guard with this woman who had found me. I didn't know enough about her, and it was up to me to learn more. I could feel the bodyguard surfacing. Quickly I remembered how to have a calculating mind that put survival above all else.

It wasn't long before the woman entered the room. I noticed immediately that I could not see her God. I wondered if it was simply my glasses or if she truly didn't have a God accompanying her. This information was crucial. I began trying to figure out how to ask her about it without seeming crass.

"You're awake." She smiled and sat down next to the bed. It occurred to me that I used to be in her role. It felt strange to be the one that was taken care of. I made a mental note not to let this woman drain herself of energy trying to take care of me. I *would* get better.

But there was no desperation here, simply care and warmth.

"How are you feeling?"

I blinked my eyes a few times, trying to wake up. Then I considered her question. How was I feeling? I couldn't even begin to explain how I was feeling. Having been through that raw period of awareness and mercifully released, I felt numb now.

I still needed to know two things: First, where was this woman's god? Second, could she tell that I didn't have one? I couldn't continue without knowing where I stood. It didn't matter that she wasn't reacting now. If she could see my lack of God, she'd want to know where he was, and I needed to know whether I could continue telling the truth or not.

Desperation mingled with my sickness, making everything hazy. The line between thought and action blurred and, I blurted out, "Where is your God?"

She cocked her head to the side, looking perplexed and slightly amused by my question. "I'm not entirely certain how to answer that."

I tried to decipher what this meant. Did it mean she had a God but had gotten rid of him like I did? Was the presence of her God painfully obvious and I just couldn't see him? Maybe she didn't know anything about Gods, so the question seemed completely inappropriate. Regardless of the answer, I needed to know. I pressed on. "Well, you have a God, right?"

Again, she look perplexed. "No. I wouldn't say I *have* a god. It seems silly to even consider *having* a god. I mean, of all things do you think you could possibly own a god? That seems utterly impossible."

Now I was completely confused. What could she be talking about? It occurred to me that not only did this woman have powerful glasses, but they were radically different than mine.

I set aside my obsession with her god status. It seemed that she was unlike the God-followers I was trying to protect myself from, and I still couldn't shake the feeling that I was safe even if I didn't know much else.

The effort it took to come to these conclusions was almost too much for me. Exhaustion swept over me again, and I let my eyes close.

The next time I woke up, I could smell food coming from the room beyond mine. I sat up and began to think through what just happened. Then I heard a faint melody and it all came back. I groaned. The pain wasn't as acute, but the ache was still there.

The godless woman came back in the room carrying a bowl of soup. "Are you hungry?"

I nodded. While I had been able to find food every now and then in my exploring, it had been a long time since I had a proper meal. She helped me get situated and gave me the bowl, then took the chair next to the bed again as I ate. "I'm scared to ask again, but I really would like to know. How are you feeling?"

I wasn't anywhere close to understanding this woman, but she wasn't like the other God-followers, and I decided that I might as well tell the truth. I took a spoonful of soup. It was a simple chicken broth, but its warmth was exactly what I needed. I sighed, content, and answered her, "Safe . . . finally." I realized I must have seemed quite strange to this woman, but I didn't care. She wasn't distressed about it, so I wouldn't be either.

"Good. It seems to be what you need."

I could feel my head nodding. Why was I so tired?

She spoke again, "I don't know if you remember the question you posed to me last time you were awake."

I furrowed my brow. I couldn't recall exactly. I knew I was concerned about her lack of God, but I couldn't formulate the words.

"I guess not," she said, releasing me from my confusion.

We sat in silence. Me, contentedly eating my soup. The woman staring off into the distance, thinking.

After a time, she turned back to me. "Is this area your home?"

A fitting question. This woman had found me wounded in what I presumed to be the middle of nowhere—well, maybe that's what she saw. Regardless, she had found me wounded and alone. It was natural that she was trying to find some way for me to make sense in this context. I doubted if that would ever occur.

"Sort of." I replied. "I used to live in a town nearby, but I left."

"Hm." She sat thinking again. "Most of the people around here aren't by themselves," she said.

"I know," I responded.

It was a pregnant silence. I knew she was going to ask. She knew I was going to tell her. I decided to just come right out with it. "I killed him."

Her eyebrows lifted in surprise, whether at my statement or the fact that she hadn't asked me directly yet, I wasn't sure. "How?"

I was amazed at her response. It wasn't "why?" or "that's impossible!" It was obvious she believed me and she didn't blame me for it. I didn't understand. "Simple, really. A dagger, straight through the heart." I said it calmly, without feeling.

"Ah," she said. "He didn't fight back?" Still she didn't ask why.

I let out an amused chuckle. "He was too far gone already. In all honesty, I didn't have to kill him. He would've just died on his own."

She nodded, solemnly, then began to talk. "I know about the gods people have here," she said, an intelligent look in her eyes. It didn't surprise me. It was already apparent that this woman had a very different pair of glasses than most people in the area. I wondered about her story.

"It took me awhile to get used to it," she continued. "I don't come from a place where gods look so human and follow people around. In fact, the whole concept of these personalized gods was rather strange to me at first."

"Was?" It was my turn to ask questions.

"Well, once I stayed here long enough I recognized that this is the way people live." She paused, thinking again. "Did you know about other people's gods before you killed your own?"

I shook my head. "No. I didn't see them. I thought my God was it. I didn't even consider that my God was different than anyone else's. When my God was sick, I thought everyone's God was sick."

She nodded in understanding. I could tell that this confirmed some theory of hers. "I'm glad I found you," she said. "It gets tiring sometimes, when everyone else lives in such similar worlds and they're so different from your own you start to think you're crazy."

"Wait," I said, recognizing the language she used. "Do you know about the Glasses Variable?"

She smiled, "Yes I do. I passed through that land before getting here," she paused remembering. "It prepared me well, I think." She turned back to me and raised an eyebrow, "I'm surprised you know the term."

"I met a man with glasses awhile back. He explained it to me."

She laughed. "There are a lot of men with glasses walking around."

It was then that I began to realize the implications of this odd conversation. It was obvious that I was missing something important. This woman did not belong here. She didn't make any sense within this context. This was a land of God-followers, and not only did she not seem to have a God, but she was living here. I assumed we were in her house. Why had a person that was notably different from the general populace settled in the area? I became suspicious. "So, what is it that you're doing here, exactly?"

I heard the remnants of her previous laugh in her answer, "I help people in their relationships with God."

My heart skipped a beat. This couldn't be possible. "I'm sorry. I don't think I heard you correctly."

"I help people in their relationships with God," she repeated, a bit more serious this time.

My eyes went wide. That was what the Man of God said he did in our town. This woman wasn't safe after all. "No. No, this isn't possible." I shifted so that I could swing my legs over the side of the bed, ready to escape. Then another terrifying thought occurred to me. "You live in a town, don't you? You brought me into another town!" I couldn't tell if it was anger or fear that was most prominent within me now.

"Wait," she said gently. "Do you want me to explain?" I realized for the first time how close she was to me in that chair beside the bed, and I began to get anxious. I had no God for her to abuse. That meant she'd be coming for me.

"No! Stay away from me." Slowly, I got up off the bed and began to back away, my hands out in front of me. I had to keep her away from my wound. "Don't touch me." My breathing had become rapid. I may have been sick, but I was ready to flee.

She could tell, but she still kept trying to coax me back, "Why do I scare you? You said so yourself, I don't have a god like the ones you've seen."

I was inching closer and closer to the door. "Neither did the Man of God. At least, I didn't see him at first. I can't believe I trusted you!" But I had trusted the Man of God, hadn't I? That's the way they all were, these people that dealt in matters of the soul. They got you to trust them with their kind-hearted nature and the way they seemed to look out for your best interests, but it was all a game, a farce. Not even they knew the terrible things they were doing to you. The melody was raging deep within me, like a scream. It was pounding away at my insides, as if trying to escape. I had to get out before that woman came anywhere near me.

It was odd that she wasn't as alarmed as I was, "Do you honestly believe I want to hurt you?"

I could feel the doorknob with my fingertips, solid, secure. Almost there. "It doesn't matter if you want to hurt me or not. It can still happen. It happened before."

I couldn't think straight. My many voices were coming back. I could hear them arguing, yelling, trying to figure out if I should trust this woman or not. I wanted to scream. All of a sudden, I knew where I was headed. All of these feelings, these thought patterns. I remembered. They were memories from the dark. I didn't want to go back, yet if I left I knew that was where I was headed. Which pain would I choose? The voices were getting louder. I was becoming paralyzed. I stood at the door, trying to regain myself.

The woman watched me, head cocked to the side like she was prone to do when she was thinking. In silence, she considered me. For some reason, the combination of her motion and the silence beckoned me, calling my gaze back to hers. She took the opportunity to search my eyes for what lay behind my fear. We stood there staring at each other

"Tell me about him," she said at last. "Tell me about the God you killed. You must have loved him very much."

Though I tried to regain myself, open the door, and flee, I couldn't. Again, this woman told the truth, just like she did when she found me in the mist. Again, she allowed me to look upon my story without blaming me for its existence. And not only had she spoken truth, she had invited me to speak it as well. "Tell me about him," she had said. She wasn't afraid of my story like the people in my town. She was allowing me to look upon the What Is I hadn't had the faith to see on my own.

Yet with that invitation, I found myself speechless. It was as if by speaking such words this woman had opened the door to the deepest chamber of my being, where the wound waited, pulsing in painful, agitated rhythm to the sickening melody that haunted me. Now that the door was opened, that melody could make its way from the wound up to the surface of myself so that it could escape in the form of a single tear. As it made its way down my face, I could feel a miniscule sense of relief. The sickening melody had gotten that much quieter. I began to wonder: Perhaps it was in tears that I could release this melody into the larger song of a bigger world so that it would torment me no longer. "I have no words," I said. But I had tears. Countless tears. Together, we let them fall.

In time, my story emerged. I told it in scattered pieces amid the tears. I could feel myself regaining faith as the woman traveled with me from the confusion about God's cough to the moment I saw the Man of God strangling him, all the way until I led myself out of the dark and finally gave myself the dagger that freed me from God yet robbed me of my home. As I spoke, I could see her reacting in the same ways I did. The frustration, the anger, the exhaustion, the deep pain. I could read them all on her face. I could feel myself gaining strength just from telling her my story and knowing I was not alone, that in fact, nothing was wrong with me. I was simply suffering from the story I had lived, a story that was real.

It was late by the time I finished, and it was obvious we were both exhausted. "I must admit," I said, "I do not understand how you can listen to my story without protesting. I haven't met anyone like you before."

She looked at me thoughtfully. I could tell this wasn't a foreign concept to her. She knew she was strange.

"Tomorrow," I pressed on, "will you tell me your story?"

She smiled. "Yes. Tomorrow."

She took my soup bowl from the table and left me with anticipation and hope. The melody was gone. It had somehow escaped and drifted away through the exchange we shared, and because of that I began to know the silence of peace. With gratitude, I let myself slip into a dreamless sleep.

Chapter 15

"I was not taught to have a god," she said the next morning as she sat by my side again. "In the land I came from, God was never mentioned. It was simply an understanding. It was not that God was absent. We lived as God, within God, recognizing God, but we did not expect God to travel with us in the way people do here. And it was too inexplicable to even bother discussing."

Her words confused me, so I set them away for another time. "You *do* have a god then?" I asked.

She shook her head, bewildered, "I still can't wrap my head around that phrase. To *have* a god. God isn't something to be had. It is to be experienced."

I waited for her to continue.

"Where I came from, it was never a matter of whether or not you had a relationship with God. That was simply assumed. The matter of God was never as concrete as a companion. It was simply an understanding that there was Something Else."

"Something else? Like something Real?"

I could see she was grasping for words. "Yes. Beyond that, it's difficult to describe. The whole thing is elusive. If you go chasing after something you know you can't understand, what else can you expect?"

I nodded.

"So that was how I lived: relating to Something Else, but never mentioning it by name. It was like dancing with mystery. Nothing was ever really certain . . . except for the things that were." She looked off into the distance with a half smile. "See, even now my words are falling apart." I sensed the deep love within her for this mysterious Something Else, an awe that was beyond need or fear, a simple heart-felt appreciation.

"One day," she continued, "I met someone with a companion she called 'God.' I was fascinated by the concept. Not only was she talking about the things we never mentioned, but her language was embodied, traveling with her. I had never thought a concept as large as God could be so contained. Yet, this person seemed so alive, so aware. . . ." Again, she struggled for words. I was beginning to recognize this as a common phenomenon when discussing transcendent things. She looked me straight in the eye. "I didn't want a God companion, but I was curious, so I left."

The ones who don't fit in go exploring. It seemed to be true.

"There are so many interesting aspects of having a God companion. It gives the mystery some substance, and I think it's helpful for many people. I have certainly learned a lot from my adventures in this land of God-followers. But as with everything, there is a dark side to putting the essence of mystery into such a small frame."

My mind immediately thought of the darker me, wondering if darkness was simply normal and not as scary as I had made it out to be.

"When I think back to the land I left and how we never spoke of God, but simply lived in the presence of mystery, I recognize that on many levels, we were protecting it. I don't think the mystery needs to be protected in and of itself, but when it is taken and embodied, it makes us vulnerable to losing sight of it."

I gave her a confused look.

"Sometimes people become so wrapped up in their God companions, they forget why they exist in the first place."

"And why is that?" I asked, truly intrigued.

"That's how they connect to something outside of themselves."

Like the bigger world the Man with Glasses talked about!

"When you told me your story about your sick God, I was not surprised. I have had so many people come to me with sick gods."

"Why?"

"This mystery, this something else, when you take the time to fully appreciate it, it's terrifying."

"I don't understand. I was always told that God loved me, that God wanted the best for me and if I just trusted in him, everything would be okay. There's nothing to be afraid of when God's around."

She nodded. It was obvious she had heard this before. "It seems to be a very safe story about God. It makes sense to you, doesn't it? It fits within your world."

I nodded slowly. "Yes. It did fit in my world before God got sick—and even after God got sick I was trying to make it fit. In fact, I'm trying to make it fit now every time I ask myself if I'm ready to look for God yet."

"So where is the mystery? Is the God you just described truly bigger than you are? Do you stand in awe of him?"

I thought about that. "Well, I could see mystery in why God loves me so much." Immediately after I said it, I felt a pulsing pain deep inside me where the wound was, almost like a warning.

She looked at me, concern on her face, "Who taught you that?"

I was confused. It seemed like a normal thing to say. Yet it hurt, and this woman seemed disturbed. "Taught me what?"

"That you are unworthy of being loved."

I never thought of it that way. "I . . . I don't know. Isn't it true?"

She closed her eyes, took a deep breath, and shook her head. It was as if she was unable to speak because of the emotion building within her. I could sense sadness, compassion, but also a flash of anger. She said firmly, "You are beautiful and very lovable. That shouldn't be a mystery."

I was taken aback by her words. I felt I couldn't accept them. All of a sudden I had become shy, and I couldn't meet her gaze. I had longed to hear those words. I needed to hear them. But I felt like I wasn't supposed to admit it.

So I shrugged off her comment, "Well, beyond that, yes, my safe story about God makes sense to me. What's wrong with God making sense?"

"If God can fit neatly into your personal world, something is fundamentally wrong."

I was glad she responded immediately. The conversation had returned to its normal rhythm.

"The whole point of God is that there is something beyond our own isolated worlds." She stopped, realizing she was getting carried away with herself. "Does that resonate with you?"

I thought for a bit, "Well, yes. If the point is to find something Real, Something Else, then how could it possibly fit in my world?"

"Exactly."

"And it *is* a bit terrifying precisely because it doesn't fit in my world. I don't know what to expect. I can't . . . control it." I was slowly beginning to piece things together.

"So, if that essence of Other is placed within the shell of a God companion. . . . "

I saw God being strangled, and it all began to make sense. "I might become scared. I might decide I want control again. I might attempt to gain control by hurting the God companion and trying to make it conform to what I want so that it fits within my world."

She nodded. "It's complex, but I love it. It's utterly fascinating. It wasn't long after I came here that I decided to devote my life to helping people learn how to maintain healthy relationships with the gods that they have. I try to help people maintain that connection to Something Else through their God companions."

"But how can you explain what happened to me? My God got sick. He nearly destroyed me. And it was other people that hurt him, not me." For some reason, the statement made me uncomfortable. "How do you know you didn't hurt him?" I heard myself say. I recognized it as the darker me, so I set the question aside for another day.

"That's the odd thing," she said. "I mentioned before that people often come to me with sick gods. Most of the time, people abuse their own God companions, but they would never kill them." She paused to think. "From what I can gather, the act of killing God would take conscious effort, and from my experience people are almost always unaware that their God companions are sick in the first place."

"Then why do they come to you?"

"They're in pain and they can't figure out why. From what I've observed, we're more connected to the infinite than we realize. I think that that there is a piece of that Something Else within us as well as outside of us, and when people lose their connection to that Something Else by abusing their God companions, they suffer too."

I shook my head. "These God companions are so weak! How can they possibly be a good way of relating to the infinite?"

"Are you suggesting that I would do better to help people kill their gods like you did?"

No. That was a painful experience. But it was necessary for me, so maybe. Yet I'd suffered so much from people trying to rid me of my god or make him "better." There was no right answer. "None of this makes any sense!" I cried.

"It's confusing, isn't it? Your story has given me a very interesting perspective into the whole matter. But in the case of all of this chasing after mystery, I think it's important to remember that none of us will ever catch it—and that's perfectly okay. We should expect to fall short of it constantly throughout our journeys. It's only when falling short becomes harmful to ourselves and to others that we need to take things into account. That's why I'm here, doing what I can to keep an eye out, helping people stay aware of themselves and what they do so that their relationships with God can be healthy, life-giving things."

"Minus the uncertainty thing, this sounds a lot like the Man of God. Actually, this sounds a lot like what I wanted to do until God got sick . . . you're one of the people in charge of this town, aren't you?"

She thought for a moment, "I wouldn't say I'm in charge of a town, but yes, I play a prominent role in one. Perhaps you could compare it to the role the Man of God played in your previous experiences."

I nodded, calculating.

"But you don't need to run away. We're not all the same, you know. And I'm certainly not a Man of God."

No, she wasn't. She was a woman without one.

Chapter 16

The next day, the Woman without a God left me alone in the house and I decided it would be a good idea to take a short walk outside. Hearing the woman's story had put me in a reflective mood, and I needed to clear my head.

The mist hadn't cleared yet. I wasn't surprised. It was a perfect representation of how my soul was feeling: shrouded in uncertainty. If I was honest, I was thankful for the mist. It kept me from seeing the town this woman lived in. Besides, I didn't want to see anything other than mist; I wouldn't know whether or not to believe it was actually there. I let out a long awaited sigh. This was my life now. God was dead, I was wearing glasses, and nothing was certain.

I kept the house in view and paced around it as I reflected on what the Woman without a God had told me. Enough of our worlds had collided that I was able to look at the most recent part of my story with new lenses. And actually, the things she said made sense to me.

Ever since I had killed God, I had been so certain I had the upper hand. I looked upon other peoples' Gods with disdain as I walked contentedly unaccompanied. The moment I had begun to feel pain, I had convinced myself that there was nothing more than my universe. I attempted to numb myself, creating the bodyguard so that I could experience as little pain as possible while being as cut off from people and their "amateur" Gods as I could. I forgot the passion in the voice of the Man with Glasses as he spoke of something Real.

Yet my attempts to keep myself from pain were futile. It wasn't the possibility of Realness that irritated my wound. It was the sickening melody that drifted into me from my dead God. In fact, it was the Realness that had brought me peace. The Woman without a God's acceptance of mystery had given her the ability to speak the truth when she saw me, instead of being burdened by "supposed to's." It was ironic how unaware I was.

I saw myself in my mind's eye, traveling in a pack, and a sense of amusement came over me. What was I doing all by myself? I knew better. I had no explanation for it, but I knew better. I had killed God, yes. But there was more to it than that. Killing God, well, that didn't actually make much sense did it? Could God be killed? If God was truly God, truly infinite, truly Real, truly beyond anything I could possibly fathom . . . I doubted I'd have any means with which to harm such a thing. It would defy me in my finitude. Therefore I couldn't possibly be alone.

Perhaps I never was. Perhaps the woman without a god was right and the mystery had been with me this entire time. Perhaps that mystery was with me as I killed that thing that monopolized my life. Perhaps that mystery was with me now. Yet I was so determined not to have anything to do with God. Why did I insist on being alone?

The answer was complexly simple: God was dangerous. Just the word held so much power. It was with that word that I nearly killed myself with exhaustion, trying to do the impossible, ignoring my own sage voice that would've had me stop for a moment to breathe, to tend to myself instead of that treacherous "God" word that took over my life and threatened my soul. It was with that word that others controlled me, told me what I was supposed to do, and I obeyed. It was with that word that others were able to reach into the deepest part of myself to hurt my soul and leave me with this gaping wound that seemed like it would never heal.

In awe, I considered the word: *God*. I considered what it meant, and I realized that when I killed God, I acknowledged the mortality of God. When abused, "God" became a dead word that meant nothing. Yes, God was dead. It was dead long before I killed him.

But I was not alone. There was something else out there. Something that "God" could have been. I could sense, deep within me, a longing for that something. It was waiting. I just needed to let myself experience it. It was time.

How desperately I wanted to take off my glasses so I could simply see! Knowing there was no hope of that, I started to ponder what it would mean to let myself become aware of something Real. If this was my world, it was up to me to make room for Something Else.

You will be safe.

The words intruded into my mind, but I knew they were exactly what I needed. If I were ever to get a chance to experience this mystery, I needed to know I was safe. I needed to know that the danger of that word, *God*, would not trick me into hurting myself again.

You will be safe.

But would I? Did I truly believe it? That familiar feeling of desperate bravery came back as I realized that once again, I had nothing more to lose. I was stuck here in the mist unless I faced my greatest fear, and I was never one to stay stuck. It was too boring. Last time, I killed God. This time, I would let myself trust something I didn't understand. I would choose to believe these words.

You will be safe.
You will be safe.
You will be safe.

I left the house behind me, allowing myself to be swallowed by the mist, led deeper into it by my sense of longing.

You will be safe.

You will be safe.

I felt a sudden urgency to remove my shoes, as if my feet needed to fully experience this journey. As if it were the most natural thing in the world, I slipped them off and cast them aside, uncaring as to whether I would find them later. I was too busy being completely present.

You will be safe.

You will be safe.

With each new step, I felt the sensation of life beneath my feet, swirling within the ground I tread. It entered my bare feet and coursed through me as I continued on, each step toward safety a source of new, ever-flowing life.

You will be safe.

You will be safe

You will be safe

You will be safe

You will be safe. . . .

Without warning, I became aware that I was not alone. There was a presence there with me. Not a human presence, like another traveler. It wasn't God either. It was both—and neither—at the same time. It couldn't be contained. It flowed through everything, a swirling, celebrating, comforting presence. I could feel it enveloping me as it enveloped everything around me. I was comforted, knowing that there was something larger than me amid it all, and because of that, everything wasn't up to me. I didn't need to do everything just right. I didn't need to see perfectly. I could simply be me.

Yet in its vastness, this presence was small enough that I wasn't forced to notice it. As the rhythm of its movement flowed throughout the world around me, I could almost lose it, left wondering how it eluded me. The more I sought to find it, the smaller it would become.

Regardless, I tried to catch it. I wanted it to be mine so I could ensure it would never leave me, but it was not mine. It was not me. It was something else entirely. I soon began to feel alone again, and I remembered what had happened: I loved God.

Then I killed him and became homeless. Now I was all that was left, and I was alone. This presence wasn't real. I probably made it up myself.

Gently, it enveloped me again. "You're asleep, Emily. This is a dream."

And for a moment, I let go. I allowed the words to seep into me, "You're asleep, Emily. This is a dream." I let myself forget everything that had happened so I could simply rest in the embrace of this steadfast, elusive presence that, I knew deep within me, had been holding me this whole time. I remembered love. I remembered what it was like not to be alone, and I remembered that this steadfast presence was real and the rest of it, all of the things I had chosen to forget in that moment, was simply a dream.

"How did you do that?" I asked in amazement.

And all of a sudden, I woke up—or had I fallen asleep again? Regardless, the presence was gone. I was still being held, but I felt like I was about to fall, and the handle of a dagger was sticking out right in front of my nose. I gasped in realization and began to struggle, but I was already falling. God was too weak to hold me. What did I expect?

In anger, I fell to the ground but immediately picked myself up and turned to face him, in shock.

"What are you doing here?" I yelled, "I thought I told you to never come near me again! I thought I *killed* you!"

Like always, God said nothing. He simply stood there, expressionless, the dagger sticking out of his chest, the blood stains decorating his clothes with violence.

"How dare you! How dare you hold me! How dare you make me believe I was safe! Why are you here?"

Again, silence.

Then I spoke, "He's always been here."

I whirled around to face me, taking in the sight of my singed hair and the blisters all over my arms that refused to heal.

"God. . ." I let the word slip from my parched lips, letting it fall like a weight from my tongue "is that a name you call him? Or is it supposed to mean something more? Do you realize he's one of us?" As I said it, I motioned to the group of me's behind me. I had split again, no doubt because God had come in and ruined everything. I looked at my faces, reflecting on the complexity I had discovered within myself during this wretched journey. Could this pathetic, weak, caricature truly be another part of me that I needed to accept?

"He doesn't look like the rest of me," I observed.

I stepped out from the crowd to join the conversation, "I don't think he's always been one of us. I think you decided to make him one of us a long time ago."

I considered this for a moment as I cried out, "But I don't want him to be part of me! Make him go away!"

I gave myself a crooked smile as I looked at myself with those dark, empty eyes. "He can stay with me. You don't have to worry about him."

I was too distraught to think it through further, "Just get him out of my sight. I don't want to see him ever again."

I watched as my blistered hand reached out for God's and the two of us walked back into the crowd, a perfect picture of pain and a tainted life swallowed up by the many faces of me. I knew banishing God was too much to ask. But I didn't have the strength to deal with it at the moment. I was weak with wonder. What had just happened? Was this truly just a dream, just a nightmare, or was that incident with Something Else simply my own wishful thinking? It had felt so real. I had felt so safe, so loved, so acknowledged for exactly who I was. And yet, it could not keep me from the arms of my dead God. Even if I was dreaming all of this, even if this horrific journey was just a nightmare, how could I possibly wake up again?

The Afterlife

Chapter 17

I was determined not to tell anyone about my experience with Something Else. This was new and potentially dangerous. I could feel my developing fragility. I was in awe, mystified, at the brink of falling in love, yet very confused. I had felt safe and loved. Why did I wake up in the arms of my dead God?

The sudden appearance of God shook me deeply. I could still see the dagger sticking out in front of my nose and feel the horror of recognition as I was carelessly dropped to the ground. This was beyond anything I could've imagined. I thought that when I killed God he would be gone forever, but apparently that was not the case. When I killed him, he just became dead. No matter what I did, he'd be with me. My stomach curdled as I recalled the large amount of townspeople who found that statement comforting. They had no idea . . .

But even as I was repulsed by the return of my dead God, I felt another even stronger stirring. When I let my guard down for that one moment and allowed myself to be embraced by that presence, something had gotten inside me. Even now, I could feel things shifting. I had yet to find out if this shifting was something good or simply someone playing with my emotions again. I wanted it to be Real. I wanted this world of multiple selves and dead gods to simply be a dream, but I was too scared of being dropped again to choose one over the other. I'd just have to live in both.

The one thing I did know was that my new experience with Something Else could easily be taken and turned into a manipulative tool. I didn't want anyone to have the opportunity to take advantage of me whether they wanted to or not. That's why I wasn't going to tell anyone about it. It was up to me to keep myself safe.

Naturally, I told the Woman without a God.

I wasn't planning on it. It just came out. The minute she walked in the door and turned to greet me I saw a light of recognition in her eyes. She knew something had changed, and I knew she'd get it out of me. I had no choice, so I told her, hoping all the while she'd tell me the loving presence I felt was Real and then proceed to give me some sound advice about how to get rid of my dead God.

She did neither.

"It sounds like it's time for you to continue on your journey," she said thoughtfully when I had finished.

"What?" I was taken aback. This was the last thing I expected. I couldn't leave now. "But . . . but . . . " I stammered. "God came back! And he's a zombie! And my wound isn't healed yet, and I don't know what I'm doing! I can't just get up and leave! I'm safe here!"

She nodded, thinking. "It depends on what you mean by safe."

I gave her a questioning look.

"From what you've told me, you've just taken a huge step forward, but you'll have to keep going or you'll lose what you've gained."

That was true. I could feel things shifting inside of me, and while I couldn't understand it, I knew they'd shift right back to the way they had been if I didn't alter something else to support the changes.

"If you stay," she continued, "you risk complacency and

laziness. If you leave, you will be confronted with the normal, healthy dangers of a human being attempting to interact with the infinite. Which would you choose?"

I responded with silence. We both knew the answer.

"What about my wound?" I asked. "Is it wise to keep journeying when my wound needs so much healing?"

She offered me a sad smile. "It's a deep wound. If you waited for it to heal, you would never be on your way. And from what I've seen of this kind of wound, it requires new experiences for healing. Truly, you have nothing to be afraid of in that regard. You're perfectly healthy."

Her last statement confused me. How could I be healthy and wounded at the same time?

She knew what I was thinking. I could tell she had faced this question time and time again. "Being healthy is not about being in perfect condition. It's about being capable of healing. You've opened up since you came here. You learned to experience your pain and to have the faith to believe that it is Real. You've learned to listen to yourself, and consequently you've experienced that Something Else. Take these things with you and use them to give yourself the opportunity to heal."

I knew what she was saying was sound, but it didn't lessen my dread. I didn't know what I was doing. I had no idea which direction I would go in once I left. I hadn't seen a fellow traveler since this woman had found me. I didn't know what to expect or how to handle the things that might cross my path. "I'm scared," I confessed.

"With good reason." She gave me a long, comforting hug that reminded me of how I felt when I was being held by that Something Else. It was strong and secure, nothing like the weak grip of God. I let her strength seep into me, and I knew that its source was deep. As she let go, she kept her hands on my shoulders and looked into my eyes with certainty and hope, "It will be worth it. I promise you."

That was what I needed. I took a deep breath. "Okay. I'm ready."

The next day I ventured forth, terrified, but willing. I stood at the threshold of the door and looked out. The mist had cleared, though there were still traces of it, reminders of the uncertainty that was part of living an honest life. I still wasn't sure what was Real, but the Woman without a God had helped me to believe my story. It gave me enough faith to acknowledge that there *was* something Real out there, and maybe I'd eventually encounter it. Much to my surprise, however, I did not see any buildings or streets. Simply forest.

I looked back at the Woman without a God, confused, "I thought you lived in a town," I said.

"I do, according to quite a few people," she smiled. "But that's not what you've seen or experienced. To you, I live in a house in the middle of nowhere."

I shook my head in wonder. Life truly was a mystery. I looked ahead of me, bracing myself for the next leg of my journey.

"You have strength within you. You wouldn't have gotten this far without it." The Woman without a God came to me and gave me one last embrace.

And with that, I took a step forward. And then another. And then another. Soon I stopped thinking about it, and I was on my way.

Within a few hours, I was lost.

It seemed useless to regard it that way. I didn't have a destination in mind and I had no path. It was virtually impossible to be lost under such conditions. It didn't matter. I was lost anyway, and I knew it.

As the morning went on, the trees had gradually become huge, their leaves creating a holey ceiling far above me. Only small, occasional strands of light were able to reach the forest floor. The area didn't seem unfriendly as much as overwhelming. I felt small. How was I to relate to such vastness?

I pondered going back, but realized I had no idea what direction that was in. I hadn't followed a path. I had simply guessed. And I hadn't seen any fellow travelers since I started out that morning. I began to sense how very alone I was, a tiny speck amid the grandiosity of this endless forest. It was becoming apparent that this was not a place where normal journeys occurred. No one following a path would get themselves here. This was a place for wanderers.

But then, I needed to wander. Things were happening too fast. I knew I had changed considerably since I killed God. I discovered that home wasn't home anymore. The Man with Glasses changed the way I saw everything. My woundedness made me aware of my own fragility. The Woman without a God helped me open up to experiencing Something Else. I couldn't process it all. My head seemed like a jumble of chaotic newness that needed to be organized and sorted through, but I refused to start the process. There was something important I was avoiding, and I couldn't put my finger on it. Wandering was my next best option.

Out of nowhere, a deafening cackle rang throughout the woods followed by a high-pitched screech that could rend anyone's ears to pieces. "I seeeeeeeeeee you," a voice said tauntingly.

So much for being alone. I could tell it was coming from above me. I found myself looking straight up into the ceiling of leaves, turning in a circle, searching for the source of the voice.

"Spinning, spinning, spinning," it rang out. "That's what you'll do. Forever and always. Spinning in circles."

I stopped moving. The statement hit a little too close to home, and I didn't want to admit it. "Who are you?" I asked, still searching the trees.

I was answered with another deafening cackle. "Does it matter? If I told you, you'd forget. Too busy spinning in circles. Tooooooo, too busy," the voice finished with an ear-piercing shriek, and I saw a blur of movement to my right. Quickly, I turned my gaze and followed it until it stopped immediately in front of me.

One second I had been following a blur of movement, the next I was staring through a pair of thick lenses into piercing eyes of ice. I could feel the hairs on the back of my neck standing on end. The source of the voice was evidently hanging off of a branch right in front of me.

When the shock wore off, I let out the breath I had been holding and took a step backward in an effort to see the rest of this presence. I wasn't sure what to expect. There was a hint of insanity in the air that gave my stomach an unsettled feeling.

I took in the sight of an emaciated woman. It looked as if she'd been living in the forest for longer than I'd been alive. I had no idea what material was clothing her because it was so ripped and encrusted with mud and dirt. Her age eluded me. If she hadn't been hanging from the branch with such control, I would've called her frail, but it was obvious she had muscle and endurance left within her. She reminded me of a spider, but with huge, thick glasses and dirty, unwashed hair sticking out in all directions. Her bright blue eyes stared straight through me as she hung there, silently waiting.

The silence confused me. It was obvious she expected something from me, but I had no idea what. I felt as if there was some unspoken rule of which I was unaware. Unsure of myself, I did the only thing I could think of: I stared back until I couldn't take it any longer.

After half a minute, I broke. "What do you want?" I asked finally.

She answered me in an unexpectedly normal voice, "If I knew, would I be here?"

For a split second I thought perhaps this person was different from the cackling blur of color previously hopping from branch to branch. This person seemed sane. Or perhaps I was the one seeing things. I felt the familiar frustration of uncertainty begin to invade my mind but was interrupted as she let out another cackle and swung herself up onto the branch, clinging to it on all fours.

"Would you?" she said in her normal high-pitched screech, extending a bony finger in my direction.

Now I was thoroughly confused. How could this woman seem sane one minute and entirely off her rocker the next? And

135 TRUE CONFESSIONS OF A GOD KILLER

whether or not she was sane, how was I to respond? I decided to adopt a civilized, conversational tone, "I know what I want. I want to find what's Real."

At first I thought she had screamed in response, but it was simply an intense, screeching fit of laughter. Besides the dull throbbing in my head, resulting from her high-pitched antics, I was weary of being laughed at.

"By ooooooowandering in the woods?" she blinked her piercing blue eyes at me.

"Listen, this is just the next step in a long journey," I attempted to explain, but she interrupted me.

"Spinning in circles. Spinning in circles. Spinning, spinning, spinning. Forever and always that's what you'll do," she chanted mercilessly. "I seeeeeeeee you."

I let out a cry of exasperation. It was obvious this woman was either totally insane or toying with me, and I didn't favor either possibility. I turned around to leave the mad woman behind when she interrupted me again.

"Do you know what else I see?" she whispered.

Her change of tone drew back my attention.

"I see *him,*" she bugged out her eyes, making it seem as if her glasses were completely blue in color and not clear at all. "He's the one. The *dead* one. He'll make you spin in sssssssssircles, circles, circles."

I stiffened. I knew immediately what she was referring to. I had almost forgotten in my confusion: God.

"NO!" I screamed before I knew what had come over me. I could feel my breathing quicken as I went into a state of panic. This was the one thing I did not want to deal with. I had sent God off with the dark part of me. That should've been sufficient for the time being. I was pretending he was gone. I didn't want to be told otherwise.

Her laugh transformed into an amused chuckle and her tone of voice changed back to that smoother, saner tone, "How do you expect to find something Real if you can't see your own Reality?"

There was someone inside my stomach, pounding against the walls of flesh. I couldn't handle this woman. I couldn't handle anything right now. I needed to escape.

I broke into a sprint, my hands ineffectively over my ears. I could hear the rustling of leaves above me, as the woman followed. It wasn't the woman I was afraid of, it was the cruel reality she pointed to. If I could get away from her I could forget about God, and everything would be okay again.

Running away was harder than I bargained for. Every step was treacherous. I had no guarantee that my feet would land solidly among the underbrush, rocks and massive roots. After five minutes of hysterical frenzy, I began to realize that it was futile to run. The mad woman had a clearer path through the trees than I had in the woods. It would be better to stop.

All of a sudden, my foot slipped, and I felt my stomach flip. In a split second I was on the forest floor, my right ankle unnaturally twisted underneath my leg. I groaned. Slowly, I pulled my leg out from underneath me and set it in front of me. I explored the pain in my ankle and assessed it as a light sprain. If I wanted, I could get up and continue, but there was no point. I didn't have anywhere to go, and it seemed the madwoman had disappeared. Where had she gone? Why were my thoughts not being interrupted by her deafening cackle?

I lifted my gaze back to the forest ceiling and searched for her, but it was of no use. *Spinning in circles. Spinning in circles.* Her refrain came back to bite me as I turned my head from one side to the other. I *was* spinning in circles. No wonder this woman had scared me. She had spoken the truth.

The truth. The word was beginning to fascinate me. I reflected back to when it was first presented to me as a cryptic code for something I never fully understood. *We know the Truth. We're committed to the Story, and we will tell others about it so they can see the Truth and be saved.* I remembered how I wanted to know what this meant, but was silently chastised for asking. Even after God was dead, the words were just as confusing.

Yet with the Woman without a God and just now with this madwoman, I had instinctively identified moments in which the truth was spoken: "You're hurt." "Tell me about the God you killed. You must've loved him very much." "Spinning in circles." And it was more than just these words. My tears as they fell to the floor of the woman's house, they were the embodiment of the Truth I had within me. Perhaps the Truth wasn't so foreign to me after all. Perhaps I knew what was true all along.

But I had run from the madwoman because of the Truth she had spoken: God. I could feel convulsions in my stomach just from thinking the word. Why had he returned? *He's always been here,* I had said. Was that true?

I took a deep breath as I realized what I needed to do next. It was time to stop avoiding the thing that scared me the most. The madwoman was right. How could I expect to find something Real if I couldn't even face my own reality?

"God?" I called. He immediately stepped out from behind a tree, eager for my attention.

I motioned for him to sit down next to me. For a while we sat together in silence. I knew God wasn't going to say anything. He never did before unless someone was saying it for him. But it was interesting just to be in his presence, to acknowledge his existence without trying to run away. I wanted to understand him so that I wouldn't be scared of him any longer.

I studied him intently. The blood on his clothes was dry now. His deadness had settled on him, and he accepted it. That's what God was about, accepting everything people imposed on him. I could probably take the dagger out of his chest and make him alive again if I wanted to. He was weak, like clay, completely moldable. It was my choice that he was dead. Death suited him, in my opinion.

It occurred to me that I wasn't actually afraid of God. It was just that I knew every time I had a chance to connect with something Real he would be there, reminding me that I could quickly turn whatever I was interacting with into something dead. *That* was scary.

"You need him right now," I said gently, sitting beside me. "He's keeping you safe."

It was an odd statement, but I accepted it in silence. I didn't need to understand. I knew now that what the Man with Glasses told me with such certainty was true: Things are the way they are for profoundly sound reasons—regardless of whether or not I knew what those reasons were. It seemed I needed this dead God to be with me . . . for now. Right now, I could take the time to question and get to know him, all the while hoping that one day I wouldn't need him any longer and maybe he'd disappear.

It was at that moment that I saw a small hand clasped in God's.

"Is there someone there?" I asked.

My head poked out from behind God's arm. "Please don't send him away. I'm scared."

Amazed, I realized I had been right. God was protecting me—or at least I thought he was. This was a symptom of my wound. The history of it was there in my fragile, childlike face.

"Why are you afraid?" I asked.

"They hurt me," I replied. "But it's all okay if God is here, like this."

It was true. If God was dead, people couldn't hurt me by hurting him. And I needed the reassurance of his dead presence. Without it, another live, vulnerable God might take his place. It was good that my dead God was following me around. In fact, I was glad to have him. I needed him.

But right as my thought completed, I recognized a tiredness in my wound, inspired by the scene before me. Then a stab of pain, deeper than my fear. I closed my eyes and listened for the message within it. *I can't live like this much longer,* it said. There was more for me to see here, but I needed to allow myself to see it. With a deep breath, I expelled my fear of further pain, then I opened my eyes and looked again.

The picture before me seemed perverted and wrong. Why was the child in me, the essence of life, seeking consolation in something so twisted? The whole scene had a tinge of gray fakery to it; the child within me, scared of itself and everyone around it, the ugliness, this dead, pathetic God that I clung to. It was all created by fear and unacknowledged pain. This was the stuff of my own personal universe. It was isolating me from the people around me. I began to wonder about that presence I experienced. If it could speak, what would it say now?

You're asleep Emily, this is a dream.

This deadness, all of it, it wasn't Real.

Yet . . . this picture before me: My wounded self and the shell of God that was left. There *was* something here I needed to acknowledge. In a flash, I saw myself with the Man of God, realizing in terror that he was holding God in a locked grip. "That's not true. It's just what you feel," he had said. And as he said those words, his hand reached for my neck so that he could strangle me as well as God. Both of us fragile vessels of the same beautiful, terrifying mystery.

The parallel was jarring.

I think that that there is a piece of that Something Else within us as well as outside of us.

This mystery, this something else, when you take the time to fully appreciate it, it's terrifying.

I don't think the mystery needs to be protected in and of itself, but when it is taken and embodied, it makes us vulnerable to losing sight of it.

In shock, I realized that just as God companions are vulnerable to the attacks of people scared by the mystery they connect us to, so are we, finite as we are, terrifying when we allow the Realness within us to emerge. To become Real, to admit to our Realness and to cultivate it, is a way of stepping out of our personal universes that goes beyond collision and merging. It is directly tapping into the Realness that we all long to be a part of, the Realness that is who we are in our deepest sense.

"I AM REAL!" It burst out of me and into the world around me. "I AM REAL!"

I looked at myself with the childlike face, peering out from behind God. I was curiously watching my outbursts, wondering, hoping. I scooped myself up from behind God and twirled.

"You are Real too," I said, tears streaming down my face.

Then I felt a cold hand on my shoulder, interrupting my joy. I didn't need to turn around to know it was God. Silently, he looked at me as if to say, "Shall I define for you what is Real?"

No longer scared of him, I was able to see that God was continuing to offer me protection. Through my happy revelations I had approached the fine line between creating another possibility for deadness and embracing something relevant. How could I say that I was Real? What did it mean?

It meant that my story was Real. When God had a cough, God had a cough. It meant that my pain was Real and the messages communicated to me through that pain were Real. But it meant something else beyond that. My pain and my story were strands of a deeper Reality. If I followed those strands, I would come to the source of who I am, the pulsing rhythm of Life itself.

You are beautiful and very lovable. That shouldn't be a mystery.

The essence of Something Else was within me. It was alive. I simply needed to acknowledge it. Somehow I had to uncover it amid the layers and layers of self that I had. There was more to being Real than simply saying it. Being Real was not as wonderful as it might seem. It was work. It was exactly what the Man with Glasses had said: a constant openness to What Is, not what's supposed to be. I needed to acknowledge each strand, each dead God and split self. I needed to travel along those strands to find the source at the heart of who I was. It was time for me to stop wandering in the woods so that I could start journeying inward.

Chapter 18

I had begun the process with God, but now I had no idea where to continue. I knew this inward journey would be difficult. The Woman without a God had said my wound was deep, and I was already aware of the vast amount of self-splitting I had done. There was so much about myself that I didn't know. I had a lot of work to do.

It seemed that a part of me understood my Realness, but it was one small part. There was more to me than that. How could I communicate this gift to myself? I decided my best option was silence. I would sit and wait for myself to emerge.

My response was more silence. It was a stubborn silence, an "I dare you to try to get me to do what you want" silence. I was angry. The rage that gave me the fortitude to stab God through the heart was still inside of me, wanting vindication and instead of direct confrontation, for which I was asking, it gave me the cold shoulder, saying "I dare you to try."

Apparently I had more to deal with than I thought. I considered stopping and trying again later, but only for a moment. I had nothing else to do. This was the obvious next step. There was conflict raging inside of me that I had ignored in an effort to survive. I needed to locate it and work it through. I understood the process. I understood where I would end up. I just hadn't experienced it yet. It was time for me to come out and face myself.

I knew the source of my stubbornness, and I plunged into its reserves, bringing up just enough sassiness to confront my coldness. "I'm just going to sit here until you tell me what's going on," I shouted, shooting a burning glare into the middle of nowhere with the hope that I could convince myself to admit what was happening. I had never directly asked myself to split before. This would certainly be interesting.

My outburst caught the attention of at least one part of me. I emerged, resignedly took a seat in front of me in a cross-legged posture, and let out a little sigh. "I don't really know what's going on either, but I agree with you that something's up. I guess we'll just have to sit here for a while."

And so I did. In silence I sat, waiting for enlightenment. As the hours passed, the group grew. Eventually I became aware of what I was attempting to do, and various different me's willingly complied. Soon there was a circle of all of me sitting on logs and on the forest floor. A few decided to climb trees and were perched, watching. Other parts were cross-legged, tensely waiting for the issue to present itself. A few of me got bored and lay strewn across each other, staring up at the leafy ceiling above me. Every now and then I would quietly murmur, "Aren't we going to get up soon? I'm tired of this. Let's go!" But enough of me was convinced that this was necessary that I remained waiting.

Then, it rained.

This did not have a positive effect on the group.

"Seriously, haven't we sat here long enough?"

"Look, she's trying to get something done here, just be patient."

"I'm wet and grumpy, and I don't care what she's trying to get done."

"Wait, what *is* she trying to get done?"

"Will someone tell me what's going on here?"

That seemed to be the appropriate question. It was immediately answered with an emotional outburst.

"I'm sick of this! I'm sick of all of this! Why am I stuck living with you? No matter how hard I try, I can't get away. Every day I wake up, and here you all are. All of us are stuck here together, and we don't even like each other! How in the world are we supposed to successfully find something Real if we don't even want to spend time together let alone understand each other? And then there's that nasty God character," I pointed in the direction of the darker me. I was sitting with my arm around God, calmly observing the group. "I killed him! Why won't he just leave? I refuse to accept him as part of this group. He is not allowed to be here, yet there he sits, staring off into space with that dark, nasty . . . "

I raised a blackened eyebrow. This was enough to encourage me not to finish my statement.

At that moment the child within me burst into sobs, "Don't talk about him that way! Don't you realize how much I miss him? And we'll never be able to get him back!"

The whole group turned to look at the last me who spoke. I had just emerged from God's previous hiding spot, and from what I could tell, I had been crying for quite some time already. My cries were immediately interrupted by one final me.

"Shut up! Just shut up! God is a horrible, nasty thing. If you miss him, you disown the rest of us. The grieving period is over. You just need to suck it up and move on—and be happy about it. We're much better off now anyway."

I ran over to separate the two arguing parts of me, frustrated that I was completely invalidating my pain. What right did I have to tell myself to suck it up and move on?

But before I could analyze any further, the child within me stepped forward, and with a strength that came from my previous acknowledgment of my Realness, I took the hand of the angry, shouting me and knelt on the ground in an act of submission. It was odd. Although it was obvious that I was giving great respect to the angry part of me from my place on the ground, I exerted an aura of inner fortitude that I did not expect. Instead of looking away, I looked up into my angry eyes, tears streaming down my cheeks, and said confidently, "I'm sorry. I'm sorry I get upset and emotional and frustrated. I'm sorry that it doesn't make sense to you that I react so strongly and feel so deeply. I'm sorry that I slow us down sometimes. I know it upsets you, and I wish I was stronger, but I'm simply not. I've tried to stop being this way, but it's impossible. This is me. This is how I am." I paused, letting the words sink in. "Would you maybe have the grace to accept me anyway?"

Taken completely aback, I stared in awe at my kneeling form as clarity of mind began to make itself known to me. Silence settled itself among us, a welcome presence after all of the shouting, griping, and emotional outbursts. It gave me the space to remember why I was so angry and gruff in the first place. My hand still in mine, I knelt with myself on the ground.

"I need to apologize as well. I know I seem gruff and heartless sometimes, but I know how fragile you are, and I don't want you to get hurt again, especially when you're still healing." I brushed a stray strand of hair behind my ear. "Sometimes I get exhausted with worry, and it seems easier to just push everyone around. I guess what I'm trying to say is, I love you, but I still need to figure out how to love you well. I'm sorry I can be such a slow learner. I'm sorry that I get frustrated so easily. Would you maybe have the grace to accept me as well?"

I didn't need to voice my response. The answer was obvious. I took my other hand in mine and, together we stood and embraced, the cheers and whoops from the rest of me showering me with love and encouragement.

Before I knew what was going on, all sorts of reconciliations were occurring. Not only had the child and the protector embraced, but the hopeless romantic had gotten into an intriguing conversation with the analytical thinker, the mother and the observer were swapping insights, and the believer in fairytales was beginning to bring energy to the tired and weary soul. I was acknowledging each different part of me and basking in the wholeness created when I simply appreciated What Is.

Finally, I was approached by the dark me. I had been waiting for this confrontation. It was inevitable, but I dreaded it. I watched those dark, threatening holes get closer and closer.

I gave myself a crooked smile. "What about me?" I asked with a hint of disdain. "Will you accept me and love me as I am?" I said it sarcastically. I didn't expect acceptance. I knew the darkness of what I had done, and that I wouldn't be able to accept it. "Will you transform me with your maturity and depth of love?" Each word was like a tiny dagger, piercing my wound.

I accepted the pain. "Yes." I looked into my dark, empty eyes. I couldn't manage any more words. I knew I'd make fun of them with my cynical remarks, and I had no interest in playing that game.

I laughed anyway. "You don't know me," I said. "You can't accept me. You can't even stomach God's presence in your psyche."

It was true. I struggled with my dead God. But I instinctively knew that this was the way of finding truth, of discovering Something Else.

"There is Realness in you," I said. "I want to accept you. Will you help me? Let me get to know you."

Again, I laughed. "You want to accept everything you've pushed away, everything you've convinced yourself was evil and wrong and unacceptable?"

I knew what I pushed away. I discovered that when I was first able to heal in the house of the Woman without a God. I pushed away pain. But pain wasn't as scary as it used to be. I discovered that too. Pain is evidence of a deeper, greater beauty. That is why it is so painful.

"You've been the closest to my wound out of all of us," I said with respect. "I need you to tell me about the things I pushed away. This is the path to healing."

I shook my head, "Think what you like, but the pain won't leave. There is too much that you don't want to see," I said, the dark holes in my eyes never ceasing in their threat to swallow me whole.

I stared back, waiting.

"Do you remember what you told yourself?" I said after a tense moment of challenge. "Do you remember when you accused yourself of keeping God sick because it was easier for you and you'd rather it be that way?" I gave myself one of my twisted smiles. "It was true, wasn't it?" A pause to let me process. "You would rather he be sick. In fact, you wanted him to be sick so badly, you strangled him with your bare hands. The Man of God taught you well, didn't he?"

I stared at myself, calculating. I didn't scare myself like I used to. Though I couldn't explain it, I felt very strongly that what I was saying made perfect sense. I tried to remember. I searched within the many different me's for the perspective I was missing.

"Here," a calm, familiar voice called out. It was the sage. "Let me help you remember. . . ."

I allowed her to guide me through my memories with her calm, accepting, perspective. I watched as God and I sat desolate on a bench in the town, the Man of God abandoning us to our pain. I watched as I picked God up and carried him with me. Then I saw us enter the abandoned shelter outside the town, and as the calm, observing sage, I entered the scene to sit and watch:

I could see myself sitting near the bed, holding God's hand, desperately pleading with him, "Can't you tell me what to do, God? I've tried everything. You're God. I know you can't possibly stay sick. There must be something I can do."

No answer.

"God!" I exclaimed, "I don't understand."

I felt the frustration come over me, the impossible conflict between letting God die and doing something heinous to keep him alive blinding me to my next actions. Afraid of the strength of my feelings, I left the room, leaving the darker part of myself behind me to do what I felt was necessary.

As I watched, fascinated, I realized that the dark me didn't have singed hair or heat blisters all over my body like I did now. Just like every other piece of myself, the dark me had been on a journey. I had a history, and over time my darkness had changed, matured, even. Now I was being allowed to see the story of my darkness. How did this dark me come to be the way I am now?

I watched as the dark me smiled, the holes in my eyes pulsing with excitement. I walked over to the bed and stared menacingly down at God. "It will never cease to amaze me how the rest of me insists on seeing you as a strong image of something real." From my observing place I flinched as I watched my unblistered hands move to his neck.

"Well, we both know better. Don't we? I've seen you manhandled by everyone else to fit what they want. Now it's my turn. I need you to get better, and you're not only going to be able to do it. You're going to be happy about it. Do you hear me?"

As always, God was silent.

"Do you remember what it feels like to suffocate? To be unable to breathe? Or should I remind you? I'm just as capable as the Man of God," I threatened. Just as the Man of God used God for his own means, so would I. Just as the Man of God strangled God, I would do the same. And where the Man of God couldn't finish the job, I would be successful.

As I continued to watch myself threaten and manipulate, instructing God on how he was to act when the rest of me came back, I saw the sparkle that I could not help but love so deeply begin to leave his eyes. This did not surprise me. I noticed the change before when I thought I had been healing him. However, as I watched through the eyes of the sage I became aware of the smallest dynamic that made an unbelievable difference in my understanding of my story. The sparkle didn't just leave God's eyes, it was swallowed whole by the darkness in my own.

As I sat there watching , I understood what the Woman without a God told me about God companions. There was a difference between God, the character who had lived with me, and the living inexplicable, relatable infinite. For a time in my life, the two, while very different things, were linked to each other, but every time I forced God to get better, a part of him ceased to be Real. By the time I finished nursing God back to health, I had reduced him to a mere three-letter word, completely under my control. It was me. I had no one to blame but myself.

"You see," the dark me's taunting truth brought me out of the memory, "you would rather God be sick than have to deal with the pain of a death you didn't plan and orchestrate yourself."

I knew I was right. I needed to face this truth. I could see the many different me's thinking extremely hard, some sitting bolt upright because of a realization or shift in views, others quietly smiling to themselves, amused, as if they'd just discovered something that had been sitting in front of their noses the entire time.

"Sometimes God dies," I said in utter amazement.

". . . and it's okay," another me completed the sentence with a sad grin.

I chuckled a bit at my own stupidity. "Except when you'd rather take control over the situation and keep him alive as long as possible."

Slowly, I started to reform my story: Death is a natural thing, and apparently it was approaching God as a natural part of our experiences together. God had been manhandled and abused so many times by the Man of God and the people in my town, that he could no longer healthily survive, let alone stand up for himself. The time had come for God and the Something Else he contained to separate, for me to mourn the loss of God and move on to new life.

But I wasn't ready. I refused to let God die. I needed the security of the way things had always been. I couldn't imagine living my life alone. In a time when I could've experienced the healing presence and renewal of that mysterious Something Else, I chose God instead because I couldn't let him go. It was funny to realize that instead of letting God die so I could embrace new life, I killed him and denied the sole purpose of his existence. I was beginning to understand why the dark part of me had such a twisted smile. The irony was darkly amusing.

Earlier in my journey, I never would've been able to face this so calmly, but I was not afraid of my corruption any longer. In fact, I wasn't surprised at all. I felt a hand on my shoulder, a weak attempt at encouragement. I turned my head to see my dead God standing there, eyes empty, face expressionless. For the first time I accepted the responsibility I had for his current existence. It was pointless for me to blame the Man of God or the group of believers for making God sick when I had done exactly the same thing. It was a human phenomenon, part of our tainted, corrupted existence. We live. We encounter mystery. Terrified, we try to control it. We suffer. And finally we become aware.

I understood now the life I needed to live. I must seek Realness. I must be willing to look truthfully upon myself and speak what is there, whether it be fear, corruption, love, or beauty. I must cultivate my Realness as well as the Realness in others, whether or not it fits the "supposed to's." I must accept my fate as a finite embodiment of mystery.

I allowed these words to sink slowly into my being. I sang them to each part of myself, hoping the tune might catch on. I breathed deeply, receiving Real, expelling my personal quandaries. Through this process, I became aware of a deep need within me.

If I was to seek Realness, I would seek peril. I had already experienced the danger of becoming Real instead of something manageable and safe. Not only had the Man of God violently attempted to control the mystery. I had done it as well. How could I survive in a world where being Real gives cause for destruction and not celebration? And even though I wished for wholeness, I was still living in my own world. How could I maintain the self-awareness I needed to remember that there was something deeper than my fears? I knew one thing for certain: I could not be Real alone.

With this conviction in mind, I got up and began my journey again. This time, searching for the people who could accept my beautiful, terrifying Realness, challenging myself to do the same for them.

It's an odd business, this human stuff, colliding worlds, a quest to find what's Real. It's complicated simply trying to communicate amid it all. I've gotten the sense that most of us, deep down, know that we're in this together. We know that it's hard and that sometimes it seems hopeless, that our journey is perilous and the path unclear even when it exists. It's because of this that we all want to help each other along, give the right encouragement and advice, point each other in the right direction.

So often, we forget that though we have so much in common in our journey toward wholeness, we cannot completely transcend living in our own worlds. More often than not, what you'd like to communicate to me gets lost in translation from one world to the next.

This is why I now believe we should spend the majority of our time simply being gentle with one another. We are all fragile creatures and it is impossible to know exactly how we affect each other as our worlds collide. Instead of giving blatant, ugly remarks of certainty and judgment, we can inquire, we can look into each other's eyes and remember that there are profoundly sound reasons why things are the way they are even if we have yet to understand. My journey has taught me that only through gentleness and compassion can we coax the Realness out of each other and into the rhythm of our colliding worlds to guide us to discover the Something Else we've been missing. And perhaps, if we allow ourselves the grace to see What Is, we will discover that what we've been losing so often in translation from one world to the next has been the same message all along.

Epilogue: Life

I cannot recall when I learned to play with the wind, but I know that wind has always spoken to me in its own odd way. Human beings always turn to wind when trying to describe the indescribable. There's something about its unpredictability and its versatility that has always reminded me of the possibility of Something Else—that beyond our often futile attempts to search for answers and explanations, maybe there is something else entirely that we haven't thought of yet. Maybe the wind carries that Something Else along with it. Maybe the wind *is* that Something Else.

So I often play with the wind. It will gently caress my face and playfully pull at my hair, and I will smile in response, acknowledging that yes, there probably is Something Else that I haven't thought of yet. And with a swift agility that never fails to cause my wonderment, it convinces me, for a brief moment, that perhaps everything I once believed in was true. It whispers in my ear. It promises fairy tales with happy endings, and all-powerful gods that never change. I revel in the old, remembering what it was like to dance through life with certainty.

But I am no longer a child. My eyes have seen too much. My heart has borne the pain of too many love stories turned sour. I

have learned how to live a tainted life accompanied by the bro-
kenness of truth-telling and the admission of the darkness
within my soul. I do not have the brute strength for certainty
any longer. I trust the meekness of my blindness instead. The
wind cannot win. Not now. Too quickly, I can catch it and call it
out on its tricks before I'm completely immersed in my past. I
laugh and I shake my head, smiling. I will never admit that I'd
like to give in to its antics. It will never admit that it doesn't actually hold stock in the things it presents to me. The game we
play with each other is much too fun for either of us to give in so
easily.

Yes, I have felt the loving embrace of an infinite spirit that
longs to wake me from my dreams of doubt and pain. But I have
also watched God become sick and die. I have witnessed and
participated in my own inner struggle to accept the corruption
within myself before I end up destroying the goodness within
me. These things have Realness too. To disown them in pursuit
of a perfect love is just as much a lie as to believe they are the only
window to the truth.

So the wind goes away in defeat, and I have won. I have held
onto my wits despite my confrontation with the representation
of mystery itself. And as I walk away, I cannot help but shake my
head in wonder.

Then, without warning, the wind returns full force, almost
knocking me to the ground as it voices its last question: "Does it
matter?" it says. After all is said and done, does it matter that I
came as close to discovering the truth as possible, or is it more
important for me to simply live truthfully, to tell my story without shame? I believe the answer is in the wind. I believe that the
wind is right when it reminds me that there is Something Else. I
haven't thought of everything yet, and I never will. But I do
know my story.

As I stand there and consider the question of the wind, I can
see the many me's standing with me, each with her own story to
tell. I want to give myself the opportunity to speak. I want to
give each part of me the opportunity to embrace its Realness. I

look at my many faces, the weary, tired soul, the believer of fairy-tales, the analytical thinker, the passionate lover, the protector, the observer, the sage, the dark one, even the dead God that might never cease to follow me wherever I go. "I want to hear your story," I say to them. And together, I continue down an invisible path, accompanied by the wind, speaking the truth I have come to know, hoping that one day I might catch a glimpse of the Something Else I have yet to discover.

Author's Note

I began writing this story as a gift to myself. My spiritual life had become so messy and complex that I could only express myself in a symbolic concept: I killed God. While the bare bones of the idea sustained me through an important time of growth, I recognized the necessity for me to flesh it out in fuller narrative form. Thus, *True Confessions of a God Killer* was born.

The story has changed, however. While when I began writing, it could have been considered an autobiographical allegory, it has undergone much editing both in concept and in form. The four-year project you are holding in your hands at this moment is fiction. I have created the characters in this story to fill roles needed to present ideas and emotions. They are not directly connected to me or people I know. I would appreciate if the reader would take that into account when embarking on this journey.

The Author

Emily Hedrick grew up in southeastern Pennsylvania. She was a book lover from an early age and fed her appetite with a wide variety of fiction later expanding into spirituality and theology. She attended Christopher Dock Mennonite High School and graduated from Goshen College in 2013 with a double major in Bible and Religion and Music with a concentration in voice.

While spending the summer after her sophomore year of college working in the Iona Abbey kitchen off the coast of Scotland, she committed some of her spiritual journey to paper. Taking her childhood love of *Pilgrim's Progress* as inspiration, her writings took the shape of this book, *True Confessions of a God Killer*.

Emily enjoys traveling, meeting new people, cooking, and enjoying a good cup of tea with friends. She is currently a member of Souderton (Pa.) Mennonite Church.

CPSIA information can be obtained at www.ICGtesting.com
Printed in the USA
BVOW02s2106030615

402847BV00006B/3/P